CW00741816

PROJECT PERSEPHONE

THE LONG RUN
BOOK 4

LEAH R CUTTER

Project Persephone
The Long Run: Book Four
Copyright © 2022 Leah Cutter
All rights reserved
Published by Knotted Road Press
www.KnottedRoadPress.com

Cover Art:
Illustration 143141902 © Tiziano Cremonini | Dreamstime.com

ISBN: 978-1-64470-313-7

Cover and interior design copyright © 2022 Knotted Road Press
http://www.KnottedRoadPress.com

Reviews
It's true. Reviews help me sell more books. If you've enjoyed this story, please consider leaving a review of it on your favorite site.

Come someplace new…
Are you a traveler? Do you enjoy exploring strange new worlds, new cultures, new people?

Journey into the various lands envisioned by Leah R Cutter.

Sign up for my newsletter and I'll start you on your travels with a free copy of my book, *The Island Sampler.*

http://www.LeahCutter.com/newsletter/

ALSO BY LEAH R CUTTER

Epic Fantasy Series

Houses of the Dead

Houses Divided

Houses Fallen

Houses Reborn

Forgotten Gods

A Wind Blown Torment

A Stone Strewn Clash

A Sea Washed Victory

The Tanesh Empire Trilogy

The Glass Magician

The Desert Heart

The Ghost Dog

Mysteries

The Purloined Letter Opener

The Tell Tale Heart Pin

Dancer in Darkness

Trophy Hunters

The Alvin Goodfellow Case Files

The Rabbit Mysteries

The Shredded Veil Mysteries

Mystery, Crime, and Mayhem

CHAPTER 1

JUDIT

Judit Kovács, Human pilot extraordinaire, captain of the crew and the spaceship *Eleanor*, was quietly, maybe even silently, swearing up a storm in her native Hungarian.

What else could she do? It was out of her hands until they reached their destination.

The countdown clock unobtrusively ticking away showed less than three minutes before they'd leave hyperspace and enter real space.

Judit was firmly strapped in, held by extensive netting in her pilot's chair aboard *Eleanor*, in the primary helm of the ship. That way, she'd be safe if the gravity went out. Or they collided with something and managed to survive. Or some other scenario that Judit had gamed out well in advance.

The chair was an architectural marvel, and despite her anxiety, was managing to keep her both cool and comfortable.

Outside the widows of the ship, no soothing points of light guided them. They weren't in a regular hyperspace tunnel anymore, but were digging across tunnels, on their way to the Chonchu system.

No one was supposed to go there. Not even the three Chonchu beings who made up the secondary engines of *Eleanor*: Eleanor, Gawain, and Abban.

Her oldest friend and pseudo-second in command, Saxon, a Yu'udir with beautiful white fur and a completely black, flesh-covered face, sat beside her. He wore his nattiest tweed vest today, a soft gray color with tiny tufts of gold and red woven in.

It would keep him cool while at the same time supposedly make him look stylish if they ended up being blown out of the sky and he had to go meet his people's god of the dead.

Judit was also dressed somberly that day, with her typical black pants cropped just above her knee, sturdy sandals, and a blood-red short-sleeved blouse.

If she was going to bleed to death in some outlandish scheme, she didn't want to see it.

Saxon looked over at Judit and casually caught her eye.

Then he said something in his native language that would have had his mother washing his mouth out with soap. Or whatever it was that the Yu'udir did when someone wished another person to be homeless and lost forever drifting across the ice floes of space. While doing something horrifically anatomically impossible.

"*Mi a pokol?*" Judit responded, wondering if the strain of this trip had gotten to Saxon and he'd finally lost it. No matter that he still sounded like a friendly, if stuffy, British English professor.

"You've been subvocalizing such astonishing curses for the last hour," Saxon said. "I thought I'd contribute one of my own."

"You're just trying to distract me from…that," Judit said, waving a hand toward the still ticking clock.

"Did I succeed?" Saxon asked dryly.

Judit sighed. She didn't sound like an emo teenager. No, really.

"We made the correct decision," Saxon said. "As a crew, coming together, to help one another. It isn't like you to second-guess yourself this way."

"I don't want to die," Judit confessed after a few more moments of watching the red numbers tick down. "And I don't want Eleanor, Abban, or Gawain to die, or to be absorbed or hurt by their queens."

That was honestly her biggest concern. The Chonchu were a hive mind. No one understood how it worked. Or what would happen when these three, after becoming individuals, got close to the queens.

Would they lose all their individuality? Go back to their core personalities with everything else stripped away? Would the queens destroy them on sight, deeming them a threat, and blow up the ship as well? Or would they be welcomed?

There were too many unknowns for Judit to reasonably plan out scenarios where she could act, could do something, could save them. They needed more information about a system that no one had access to.

The system that they were about to arrive in less than a minute.

"You know that I love you, right?" Judit said. She had to tell Saxon, her one true best friend, that sentiment, at least one more time.

"I know," Saxon said. "There's no one but you who I'd want to be at my side when the final battle begins."

"Weirdo," Judit said teasingly. Yu'udir myths from their home world had some sort of apocalyptic end to everything, involving endless wars.

"Furless freak," Saxon said affectionately in response. "Though I did wonder if you were trying to get on my good side by not shaving your legs. Again."

"I shaved my legs!" Judit said hotly. "I depilated everything chemically before we started this trip."

"Really," Saxon said dryly. "Then didn't bother bathing afterward?"

"What?" Judit screeched. "You flea-ridden, excrement filled bag of—"

"Normal space breached," Abban's voice said softly over the ship's comm.

Judit snapped into focus, reaching for the pilot's yoke in front of her.

She and Basil, the , the Oligochuno and ship's main engineer, had spent time wresting navigation control away from Eleanor and the others, so that Judit had some piloting abilities and could direct the ship from the primary helm.

She gave a sigh of relief when the ship responded to her controls and she was able to fire up the primary engines, sending them in the right direction.

"Where are we?" Eleanor asked as Saxon started his own work as a navigator.

They'd deliberately tried to come in on the "far" side of the system, as it were. If the sun of the system was in the center, with the hyperspace gates on the "western" side, they were supposed to arrive on the "eastern: side. It would take them a few days slow travel to get to the home world.

"Not exactly where we'd planned," Saxon grumbled. "We're a little north of the spot we'd chosen, on that plane, though, and just as far away from the main planet."

"Good," Judit said. "Basil? Any issues with the engines?"

"None so far," Basil said. If Saxon sounded like a British professor of literature, Basil had a weedy twang to zir voice, like a typical nerd. "All the new coolant tubes held nicely. No, wait. There's a leak. I need to go fix this."

Zie signed off in a hurry. Judit sighed. Hopefully it wasn't bad.

"Menefry? Any hidden weapons aimed our direction?" Judit asked as the ship glided along.

The Khanvassa who worked as their security expert replied first with a short melodious phrase in his native language, which Judit knew was a quick prayer to his Goddess Nesnefera, thanking her for their safe arrival.

"I cannot sense any weapons pointed our direction," he added. "No abrupt heat signatures in the area. Nothing suddenly powering up."

"Good. Thank you," Judit said. "Kim?"

"We made it!" came the cheerful reply. "See? I knew nothing bad would happen to us on the trip here."

Judit rolled her eyes. The Bantel were notoriously cheerful (all right, so Judit would say *obnoxiously* so). Though no one had ever been able to prove that the Bantel had a magical ability to see into the future, their "gut feelings" tended to be right more than average.

"What about the chatter in the system?" Judit said, directing Kim to her actual job as communications expert.

"Oh! Right," Kim said. "It's all quiet." She paused. "It's a little too quiet. I would expect more chatter between the planets. There's very little talk going on. Huh. What's that?"

Judit tensely waited for Kim to say more. After a few moments, Judit asked, "What is it?"

"We're being hailed. I think. Weird old-timey setup. Direct beam," Kim said distractedly.

Judit didn't ask for anything more, letting the person do her work.

Kim, for all her cheerfulness, eye-searing outfits, and skin colored to clash, could be a professional.

Judit just had to step back and let Kim do her job.

"There it is! Gotcha!" Kim said enthusiastically. "Uh oh. You better hear this."

"Put it ship wide," Judit directed. This wasn't the sort of thing that she wanted to hide from her crew.

"Alien ship," came a low, mellow, female voice. "You are in violation of the trade agreements between the Chonchu queens and the Cartel. Explain your presence here."

"Our shipmates needed to come home," Judit said out loud, trusting that Kim would transmit her words.

She didn't want to go into any details about how they were an escaped ship from *Camelot*, possibly the only of Arthur's experimental fleet to survive the destruction of the space station.

"We are sending a ship for you," the mysterious voice suddenly announced. "If this is a trap, you will be destroyed without warning."

"That's it," Kim said. "There's no more transmission."

"Thank you," Judit said. "Let me know immediately if someone calls back. I don't care if I'm sleeping, working out, taking a shower, what have you. Got it?"

"You betcha!" Kim said.

Judit knew that if she kept rolling her eyes at her crewmate that she'd eventually pull something.

After a moment of debate, Judit finally called out, "Eleanor?"

No response.

"Abban? Gawain?"

Ominous silence returned her call.

"I think we have a problem," Basil said suddenly.

Judit stripped the netting off of her and stood up, stretching slightly. "I'll be down in engineering," she told Saxon. "Let me know when our ride shows up."

"Will do," Saxon said. "Now comes the easy part, eh?"

Judit felt like giving him yet another piece of her mind, swearing at him for saying such a thing.

She knew he was only trying to cheer her up, though.

"Yeah, right," she said sarcastically as she left the main helm.

What else could go wrong? They were in a completely forbidden part of space, and though she had some navigation capabilities, they couldn't get out of the system in the usual manner, that is, through hyperspace.

They were stuck here, and facing an incredibly long run if anything went wrong.

CHAPTER 2

BASIL

LIKE THE REST OF THE CREW, BASIL UNDERSTOOD THAT there were potentially horrible consequences to their actions, coming into an alien territory unannounced, through the back door, as it were.

However, of all the crew, zie also felt the best about their decision. Zie fully believed Eleanor, Gawain, and Abban when they said that their queens wouldn't attack the ship, wouldn't kill the crew outright. No, Judit and the rest would have to do something threatening to elicit that sort of reaction.

Zie hadn't been worried about zieself or the rest of the crew.

All of zir worry had been reserved for the three beings who made up the secondary engine: Eleanor, Gawain, and Abban.

What had happened to them?

Of course, as soon as they arrived, one of the coolant pipes started leaking. At least it was in an obvious place. The slightly blue-green algae that made up the viscous biological liquid dripped down the wall to the right of the door inside the secondary engineering room.

Basil had everything in place, having fixed many of these pipes before. Zie had a specialized ramp that zie could adhere to, which got zim up, toward the ceiling. As a pseudopod, zie could grow as many limbs as zie needed. For this repair, zie currently had five arms: two for keeping zim solidly on the ramp, one for scraping away the old coolant as it continued to ooze, one for holding the bucket with repair liquid, and the last for actually brushing on the patch material.

As the material hardened and the hole stopped leaking, Basil looked back and gave the entire area a good once over.

The Oligochuno didn't have eyes, but an orange sensing ring that encircled their entire head. Zie didn't *see*, not in the sense the Humans and other races used. Instead, zie *sensed* things. In addition to visual, zie also smelled the chemical structure of the area and so was able to tell if this fix would hold, or if zie was going to have to replace the entire pipe. (Not yet, but soon.) Zie regularly saw heat signatures as well, though minute shades were only notice-able if zie was concentrating on them. (So zie wouldn't notice a flush of anger unless zie was looking for that sort of thing.)

Everything on the wall in front of zim looked stable enough for the time, so zie turned back around, glancing at the amber spars that encased the three beings who made up the secondary engines of the ship.

And froze, all the segments of zir body stiffening. Zie balanced precariously on zir ramp for a moment, nearly falling over, before zie recovered zieself and hurriedly inched down, then over to the dais where Eleanor, Gawain, and Abban stood.

The three amber spars no longer had any light glowing from within them. They'd all gone dark.

When Judit called their names and they didn't respond, Basil told Judit to get down there.

Someone else needed to witness what zie was sensing.

Basil had never been able to sense the organic beings encased in the amber. Now that they'd grown dark, zie realized that at some level, zie had been able to sense *something*. A presence, perhaps.

That was very much missing.

Zie felt zir segments align a bit more when some of the tiny lights inside of the amber blinked. Each spar had at least a dozen or so, each flashing in its own sequence, with its own heartbeat.

When zie measured, zie concluded that those tiny lights maintained their usual order of beats, just slowed down to about a quarter of what they'd once been.

"*Az isten nevében!*" Judit proclaimed from the door. "What happened to them?"

"I don't know," Basil said sorrowfully. "They were fine when we first came into the system. Then I had to fix that leak. When I turned back around, they were like this."

Judit approached the dais slowly, as if she was afraid whatever had happened to the three beings who ran the secondary engines was contagious. She jumped when the first lights blinked.

"Is that good?" she asked, glancing back at Basil.

"I believe so," zie said. "It's as if their systems have been slowed down."

"Hibernation," Judit said grimly. "Okay. We can work with that."

Basil suddenly felt better. Judit, of course, had thought about this, and possibly had a plan of action for it.

"It'll be okay," Judit said softly.

At first, Basil thought that she was addressing zim. But all her focus was still on the three Chonchu.

She completed crossing the floor of the secondary engine room and reached out, placing a hand on the lumpy side of the tallest spar, the one that encased Eleanor, back behind the other two in the lop-sided triangle that they formed. Judit and Eleanor were close to the same height, about one hundred and seventy centimeters tall.

Judit stroked the spar a couple of times, running her fingers gently across the uneven surface.

Basil had done the same more than once, particularly while trying to fix the nutrient supply that the three used, making sure that the ingredients that zie was adding were helping and not hurting. The spars had a slight heat to them, in addition to the light they generally emitted.

As far as zie could tell, their chemical makeup remained the same. The composition of the three spars hadn't changed.

They were just no longer conscious.

"We'll get you back. Wake you back up," she said firmly. She reached out and now touched the other two, Abban and Gawain, stroking her fingers across them as well while she talked.

"You're part of my crew," Judit said, addressing all of them. "And no one messes with my crew."

Though it was a Human and Yu'udir expression that Basil had had to teach zieself, zie still found zieself smiling at that.

Yes, Judit would find a way to return Eleanor and the others to what she considered their rightful place, here on the ship.

Or else there would be hell to pay.

CHAPTER 3

SAXON

Saxon sat by himself in the primary helm while Judit went to check on the others, first the three beings who made up the secondary engine (who appeared to be completely frozen now) and then on Kim and Menefry, in the other helm.

The primary and secondary helms looked very similar, with golden couches that perfectly fit whatever race was utilizing them, a broad window out the front showing the stars and the distant sun and planets, soothing green walls that spoke of spring, and a rubbery black floor that provided a good grip. Soft lights blinked on the console, assuring him that at the very least, the mechanical aspects of the ship were all running.

He appreciated the time alone, more so than he'd ever admit. His heart was still sore from all the loss he'd experienced in the past few months. First the destruction of *Camelot* and the dreams that Arthur represented, not just for the Yu'udir but for everyone looking to get out from under the yoke of the Cartel. Then the loss of his brother. Though his sister hadn't banished him from his family, she had cut him loose.

Part of why he'd agreed to come to the Chonchu system was because he didn't have anywhere else to go. This ship was now his home. Judit had always been the star he'd hitched his soul to.

He knew that she never would have abandoned any of her crew when they were in need. She hadn't for Kim, for him, and now, for the most alien members, she'd brought them back to their home system.

She'd see that they were all taken care of, to the best of her abilities. Or avenge them if something went horribly wrong.

Saxon continued to passively scan the system they'd arrived in. It would take them about two and a half days to reach the home world from where they'd come out of hyperspace. He assumed that it would take that long for whoever had first hailed them to do the same.

So he was quite astonished when a loud ping interrupted his contemplations. It had only been three hours since they'd arrived.

What was that approaching them?

It was big. Not space station large, but bigger than most of the freighters he'd ever seen.

And it was moving fast. Directly toward them.

He had to assume that if they could start that fast, they could slow down before they collided.

"Judit, I believe our friends have arrived," Saxon told her.

"On my way," Judit said. She sounded slightly out of breath.

When she came barreling into the helm, Saxon understood why. She'd taken a break in the ship's gym, probably pounding the hell out of one of the punching bags, releasing her tension and aggression that way.

He hoped that she'd bled off enough. It wouldn't do for Judit to be too hot under the collar when they met whoever was coming to greet them.

"What the hell is that thing?" she asked even before she slid into her pilot's chair.

"I'm not sure," Saxon admitted. "I've never seen something like that before."

"Duh," Judit replied. "What else can you tell me?"

"It's not all metal, or ceramic," Saxon said, quickly sorting through his readouts. "The ship, itself, appears partially organic."

"Huh," was all that Judit could say. "I'm assuming Chonchu? Kim? Any word? Have we been hailed again?"

"Not a peep," was Kim's chipper reply.

Saxon watched as Kim pinged the oncoming vessel aggressively. Rudely, even, which wasn't really her style. But it was still bearing down hard on them and they didn't know what to expect.

He would have likened the ship to one of those huge aquatic animals that Humans had on Earth, and had transplanted to their other worlds as well: sperm whales, the kind with the flattened face and long blocky body. Almost like a huge shipping container, though with rounded edges.

The ship itself had few running lights, but what Saxon could see in the visual spectrum was a dark gray, the hard fog of a fall night, creeping across hunting fields and hiding enemies. Its skin appeared to be mostly featureless, no divots or protrusions along the smooth, curved sides.

There wasn't a square angle on the entire ship, not even at the tail which tapered off gracefully. While *Eleanor* wasn't a huge ship, the one facing them could easily fit a couple of dozen *Eleanors* inside of it.

"Got a message!" Kim said exuberantly. "'Stay where you are.'"

"Alien ship, what is your intention?" Judit asked.

Saxon could hear the strain in her voice.

Menefry spoke up. "We have no offensive capabilities," he softly reminded everyone. "We could possibly blast a tiny asteroid out of our path. That's about it."

"Alien ship, please respond," Judit said again. She turned to Saxon. "Start a timer. If they don't respond in five minutes, we're out of here."

Saxon nodded and reset the countdown clock.

The alien ship loomed silently ahead of them, growing bigger by the second, blocking out the light of the sun behind it.

Seconds counted down.

"Everyone, get strapped in, ready for evasive maneuvers," Judit announced to the crew. "That includes you, Basil."

Saxon kept his smile to himself, hearing the Oligochuno already grumbling about having to strap down zir tail. The last time they'd been in a simulation and Judit had begun evasive maneuvers, zie had only strapped in what effectively worked as zir torso. Then complained for three days about the bruises the rest of zir body had suffered.

To support Judit, Saxon did a thorough scan of the area, making sure that he had placed every single hazard or spec that might get in her way as she went *zoom*.

"Alien ship," Judit said one last time. "We are about to begin maneuvers to leave the region and get out of your path."

No response.

"Don't say I didn't warn you," Judit added. "And *az ördög vigye el*," she muttered. "Menefry? Any signs of weapons powering up?"

"Negative," Menefry said. "If that ship has guns, beams, or cannons they're all well-hidden."

"Starting evasive maneuvers now," Judit said as she pulled hard and twisted the piloting yoke.

The view of the massive ship in front of them shifted down minutely.

Then *Eleanor* stopped moving.

"Basil! Why have I lost all maneuvering power?" Judit growled. She pulled the steering yoke this way and that, but Saxon could tell the equipment was unresponsive.

"My boards show that you are still fully in control," zie said.

"I can't steer. I can't power us out of here. I can't do *anything*," Judit said.

Saxon had never heard his captain so close to losing it.

A seam appeared on the face of the ship bearing down on them, running across the entire width.

It slowly hinged open, revealing utter darkness inside.

"Menefry! Fire what we have," Judit directed.

Nothing happened.

"My controls are frozen," Menefry responded after a few moments. "We are in the hands of the Goddess, now."

That was *not* the right thing to say to Judit, who firmly believed that she was the sole pilot of her destiny. "Everyone evacuate to the escape pods," she said.

"I don't think that would be a good idea," Basil countered. "My boards say that just about everything other than life support is no longer under our control."

"How did they disable us?" Judit demanded to know. "Is there some sort of beam that they've activated?"

"Negative," Saxon, Basil, and Menefry all responded at once.

"It's Eleanor," Basil added. "And the others."

It took Saxon a few moments to realize what Basil was saying, that he wasn't talking of the ship but the being.

Though Basil and Judit had rewired some parts of the

ship so that Basil would have control, Eleanor must have overrides that they hadn't been aware of. He remembered Basil's report, talking of the organic wires that had started showing up in the conduit tubes, beside the inorganic ones.

The three beings who ran the secondary engines now also ran the rest of the ship.

And they were offline.

"Get strapped in again if you've unhooked yourself," Judit warned everyone as the dark mouth drew nearer. "We may be in for a bumpy ride down the gullet of this thing."

Saxon nodded. While his people didn't have the myth of being swallowed by a whale, they did have other creatures, such as the dragon-like monster who ate the sun during the battles at the end of the worlds.

Into the darkness they went.

Hopefully to plunge through and come out the other side whole.

CHAPTER 4

SACHIKO

Sachiko had ignored the invitation the first time it had arrived, many years before. And the next several after that.

Her? Teach at a spy school, set up by the Cartel?

Why in the name of the seven hells that her grandmother had sworn by would she do something like that?

She'd never had children. Or family, for that matter. She had people she hired temporarily for crews, along with competition. Her jobs came from referrals.

And that last job—destroying *Camelot*—had set her up for life.

She'd never have to take another job. She might, though, just to keep her hand in.

But for the first time in her life, she could play the part of a dilettante. She could own the island she currently resided on, with its sparkling amethyst-colored sands and tropical breezes. She spent her time lying on the beach on a mat, soaking up actual, real sunlight, attentive servants standing behind her, awaiting to serve her every need. The tablet lying beside her had every imaginable entertainment on it. The villa she stayed at had the best virtual reality suite she'd ever experienced.

She had everything.

But after three months, Sachiko was slowly coming to realize that she needed something else. Something *more*.

She'd always defined herself as the best at whatever she did. Was she now merely the best at lying on the beach?

That silly invitation nudged her again.

She knew she shouldn't. There were so many reasons why taking this gig was a bad idea.

People would *know* her, afterwards. Not just rich people with power, who would be useful to her. But smaller people. School administrators. Faculty. Students.

Sachiko had always considered herself self-contained, perhaps to an extreme. Isolation didn't bother her.

Except when it did. When it appeared to chafe her like an ill-fitting environmental suit.

She could never, *ever* admit to her most recent job. Could never allude to it. No one could associate her with that project. There wasn't a system who would shelter her if that news came out. No disguise would be good enough.

Yet, she found that she somehow needed to take credit for it. It was illogical. Suicidal, even.

However, who would believe a student in a spy school? They'd obviously been duped by their teacher.

Yes, there had to be just one such individual who could be hinted to. Then, if necessary, be made to disappear afterward.

They had chosen a deadly occupation, after all.

Sachiko chuckled to herself and rose from her mat. She was nude on her private beach, able to walk directly into the soothing waters, then not have to worry about a wet suit afterward.

But instead of heading toward the water, she walked

directly back into the cool shade of the villa, already composing the letter in her mind, listing her demands, what sort of privacy and protection she'd expect.

They'd expect her to come back, of course.

Maybe she would. Make an annual pilgrimage to the school. Allow herself to be seen, at least once a year.

Just the thought soothed her ego. She hadn't even realized that she'd had such, not until now. She'd thought just herself taking pride in her work was enough.

But it wasn't. Not really. Not anymore.

However, it truly didn't matter. She could always quit the guest lecturer position if it became a burden.

Then track down and kill every single one of her students.

That might be a fun game, after all.

CHAPTER 5

MENEFRY

ELEANOR LOST POWER AS IT ENTERED THE BELLY OF THE beast.

Darkness consumed them.

Menefry softly sang a prayer to the Goddess, firmly placing not just his fate but the fate of the crew in her many hands.

Slowly, lights came back on. Both inside the ship as well as outside.

They floated inside a large area. Menefry studied the features he could see from where he sat in the secondary helm, as scans were still useless. He heard Judit cursing as she felt the ship touched down gently, the landing as softly as the sigh of the Goddess on the wind.

He didn't see any weapons. In fact, he would bet that they'd just landed in a cargo hold. The walls were the same industrial gray that Humans favored, though the lights were on the bright end of the spectrum, cold, with no warm sun tones. Over on the far side were what looked suspiciously like standard shipping containers.

"Air is breathable," Saxon announced. "Gravity is a little light. Temperature is twenty degrees Celsius."

Menefry gave an automatic shiver. He was going to be cold there. Good thing he was already dressed warmly, in his heaviest brown vest and black pants.

Kim, on the other hand, looked like a delicate puffball. If they came in that range of colors, from a light pink to a dark blue, all of it electric. Instead of regular fabric, she wore something more akin to fur, with all the strands standing on edge ten centimeters up from the surface. Her skin was a particularly bright shade of green that somehow managed to clash with all the other colors, while her eyes were a bright gold.

"We're here!" Kim chipperly announced to whoever had been speaking with them.

Menefry just shook his head. Though he knew that his friend might be scared, she was also looking forward to the adventure they were about to embark on.

It would be up to him to protect her from the dark.

At the far end of the cargo space, a door opened. Half a dozen beings came through.

Chonchu.

The front three Menefry would guess were the actual greeting committee. They were all tall, something that Menefry hadn't realized until he'd started studying the race, as tall as a Khanvassa, so nearly two hundred twenty centimeters tall. (The three beings in the secondary engineering room were much shorter.) Thin, though, their skin a pasty white, like a grub. They wore gauzy, shapeless fabric draped over their torso, pinned here and there to hold it.

He heard Kim draw in a breath. It took him a moment to see it as well.

The fabric, in this light, had an opalescent shimmer, like dew drops from the passing of the Goddess.

He knew that Kim was already planning outfits made from it.

They were bipedal, with large black eyes that held no discernible pupil and dominated their face. No nose to speak of, or lips, either. They tended to walk with their mouths open, showing delicate pointed teeth.

While the front three were there to meet them, the back three were probably their equivalent of muscle. Unless they had alien technology that Menefry had never seen, he was certain that he could take all of them. Even if their minds were linked and they would attack simultaneously.

"Let's go meet them!" Kim said, springing up out of her chair in the secondary helm.

"I will go first," Menefry said. If they attacked, well, they would learn that they had to go through him in order to get to the rest of the crew.

"Negative," Judit said.

As Menefry knew that she would. She was the captain. It was only appropriate for her to be in the center of everything.

But he would be at her side, ready and armed, prepared for the first sign of danger.

———

AFTER THE CREW HAD WALKED OUT INTO THE HUGE echoing cavern of a space, and introductions had been made, the Chonchu started questioning them.

They hadn't given themselves names. Menefry understood that Eleanor, Gawain, and Abban were different from the rest of their race, in that they understood that there was an "I" to speak with, not merely a "we."

Menefry listened to the talk with only half an ear, as he continued to scan the area, making sure that no one was about to sneak up on them, to take them hostage without a fight.

The three behind the greeting committee watched him the most out of all the crew, at least as far as he could tell. When a lull occurred amongst the other players, one of them spoke directly to him.

"How many weapons do you carry?" he—she—zie—asked. The voice had deeper tones, more like Gawain than Abban. The three in the greeting committee, based solely on the timbre of their voices, Menefry would gender as female.

"Many," he replied solemnly. He couldn't read their faces. They didn't have much in the way of expression. However, the Khanvassa expressed a lot of their emotions with their more delicate second set of hands.

While the Chonchu only had two hands, instead of six, they still appeared to express things with their arms and fingers.

Was that a tightening of the hands he saw? No fists, but still a stiffening?

"You will not hurt my crew," Menefry added, just to see what the reaction was.

Interesting. The joints appeared to relax at that, the fingers wiggling.

"How do we know you are not spies? Sent by The Universal Trading Cartel?" the individual asked.

That must be shock, the way all the individuals around the speaker stiffened up, hands frozen, arms stiff. On one, even the shoulders tensed.

Kim spoke up. "Pffft. The Cartel. I'm always looking for ways to line my nest. I'll take pretty much any job. Except ones with the Cartel."

Menefry suspected that just clouded the skies instead of clearing them.

"We're here for our crewmates," Judit explained again.

"The three Chonchu who make up the heart of *Eleanor*. They won the lottery run back here, to be part of the experimental ship program that Arthur, the Yu'udir, was running on *Camelot*, the space station. They needed to be back in contact with their queen."

Though Judit had said all of that before, it finally appeared to sink in with the greeting committee.

"You escaped the destruction of *Camelot*," the center one said. She was the tallest, dressed in fabric that had more green tones.

"We did," Menefry said, drawing attention back toward him. "And now, the Cartel is hunting for us. For our ship. For our crewmates."

"Protector," one of them called him. "You do not care for the guidance The Universal Trading Cartel brings to you?"

"They do not speak truly," Menefry said. "They do not have the voice of the Goddess. They are false."

One of the three in the back laughed. The sound reminded Menefry of Abban and zir abrupt, "Ha! Ha! Ha!" The tone grated, yet at the same time, Menefry knew the humor was genuine, that this one might travel the Path of Laughter.

"They are like us," zie proclaimed, stepping forward. Zie had the same nasal tone that Abban did, neither male nor female but like an undecided pupa, who hadn't grown into their shell.

Strange. The others parted and slid around behind zim, as if to give zim zir proper place among them.

Alone, with the rest surrounding zim.

Zie had the most gold in zir fabric. Zie was also the shortest in the group. Zir fingers were webbed, and sharp golden claws tipped the ends.

Suddenly, the entire group stilled. It was as if a cold wind had blown in from the desert, carrying unidentifiable scents that struck fear into the hearts of all.

When they came back to life, it was as if warm water had bathed them, relaxing all their muscles. They didn't smile, unlike a Human or Yu'udir. But their fingers wiggled, as if flowing freely in a stream.

"Belaitha would like to meet with you," zie said.

As a group, the Chonchu turned to go.

"Who?" Judit called after them.

The one in gold came back. "The nearest queen. Belaitha." Zie paused, head tipped to one side, as if listening to a sound that only zie could hear. "She says to tell you that you are safe here. Even as we approach the home world, no one can detect you. Or your ship. The Universal Trading Cartel cannot find you here. No one can."

Just before they reached the door, zie called back one last time. "We'll be there in an hour!"

Then the Chonchu walked out and Menefry had as many questions as he'd had at the start of this.

Perhaps more.

CHAPTER 6

KIM

KIM WAS CERTAIN THAT SHE WOULD *ROCK* ANY AUDIENCE with a queen. Just look at her! She had on the most amazing outfit with all the colored fur. And her skin was such a pretty green. She'd chosen that color specifically because it was similar to the color of pictures she'd seen of the sea on the Chonchu home world, so it would make the Chonchu feel more comfortable with her.

While her eyes didn't really match—they were just a gold color—she'd always thought that that particular shade made her look wise. Plus, it was the color of gold and all the pretty metals that were only valued for their looks, as they were too easy to manufacture to have any worth these days.

"A queen!" Kim exclaimed as she bounced along. Okay, so maybe she'd said that more than once, given the eyeroll that Menefry gave her.

"May she be guided by the Goddess and listen to her wisdom," Menefry intoned in return.

"Fine, fine, whatever," Kim said. "Do you think I should get Basil to make me a crown? Or would that be pretentious? Do you think she has a crown?"

Menefry appeared to give the question some actual thought. "Given the flatness of their face, and the crest at the front of their head, I would think that crowns would be distinctly uncomfortable for the Chonchu," he concluded.

Kim sighed. She might get Basil to manufacture one for her anyway. Just to shake things up a bit.

Or maybe she could steal one? Surely if the queen had a bunch of them, she wouldn't notice if one went missing, right?

Because there sure wasn't a lot to steal around here. The cargo bay they'd been dumped in didn't have anything interesting in it at all. And Judit wouldn't let her go and explore the few cargo containers sitting in the corner. Just to see what they were sharing space with. Might be dangerous. Better to just peek inside one, right?

But no. Judit as well as Menefry had put the kibosh on that.

It was odd not being able to see where they were going. There weren't any windows in the danged place, at least none in any of the space that the crew had been brought to. Just long, skinny corridors with high ceilings because the Chonchu were *tall*. Kim barely came up to mid-chest on most of them.

Though the fabric they wore was really pretty. She could see making something sleek out of some of that. Easy enough to get her skin to change to that color as well. She really liked how it shimmered.

After yet *another* corridor, this time though it was through an airlock and off of the first ship, the one that had swallowed them whole, and onto another.

Finally, they were someplace that at least *felt* interesting.

The temperature on the first ship had been cool. Saxon had been digging it, but to be honest, Kim and her people preferred a slightly warmer temperature. This place was much warmer. And humid, in a way that spaceships generally weren't. The air smelled of the sea, salty, with a hint of green seaweed at the back of it.

In addition, instead of plain gray walls, everything was now painted black. Not a matte black, though, something shiny. With tiny bits of iridescent something scattered through it. It was kind of like the sky at night from a planet, though none of these "stars" stood out.

The first ship had been utilitarian in the floor and lights. This place wasn't opulent, but it was nicer. Strange, it didn't have straight angles anywhere, not where the floor met the walls, or the walls met the ceiling. It wasn't a round tunnel that they walked in, but everything had been softened.

The light remained bright, though, that harsh white that did nothing for the green of her skin. She'd considered lightening the color up a bit so that it shone more, but decided to wait until they reached the audience hall. She'd only do it to impress the queen.

After just a short walk, two grand doors stood closed in front of them. Thinking back, Kim realized this was the first "art" that she'd seen. The doors had what looked like embossed golden columns running up and down them. Were those red touches running around the capital and the base rubies, or some other sort of gem? Blue-green vines grew in the spaces between the golden pillars.

Wait—those weren't painted on. Or they were a really good holograph, with the leaves slightly swaying in whatever breeze.

"We will wait here," said one of the group of Chonchu who'd accompanied them to this point.

"Thank you," Judit said.

Kim could tell that Judit was still pissed off at being here in the first place. Not because the captain resented the trip or needing to do things for Eleanor, Gawain, or Abban. No, because she hadn't been told anything and she was frustrated with the lack of intel.

Maybe Kim had been hanging out too much with Menefry, because she figured that at this point, they just had to go with the flow. Follow the path of the Goddess, you know?

Until they could figure out a way of freeing themselves from this place. And stealing something cool.

The doors silently swung inward. Darkness filled the space beyond them.

Kim felt the way gravity fluctuated at the doorframe. As a Bantel, she was more in tune with that sort of thing than the others. The amount of gravity hadn't changed much. It was just slightly lighter in here.

Wherever *here* was.

As far as Kim could tell, they were standing on a balcony, sticking out into a huge empty, echoing space. A golden rail, coming up to waist-high on the taller beings, chest high for her, enclosed the space. Beyond that, Kim saw the telltale flash of an energy shield.

No one would be shooting anything through that. Probably no projectile weapons either. Someone trying to heave themself off the balcony would probably get a nasty shock as well.

Interesting!

She was already trying to come up with schemes for how to subvert all this security when a deep bell sounded.

Menefry stiffened beside her. She put a comforting hand on his hard shell, nodding.

Though the bell hadn't been loud, it had still reverberated through her bones.

It sounded to her like the calling of the faithful to prayer.

Or the summoning of a queen.

Lights came on to either side of them.

This place was *huge*!

It was like the entire center of a space station, one that went up and down, that had been completely hollowed out. Kim was having difficulty judging how far away the opposite wall was. Five hundred meters? A thousand?

Like everything else, the space was rounded, no corners or sharp edges.

Kim gasped when she looked up. A rounded dome covered the ceiling, the gold color matching the spars that encased Eleanor, Gawain, and Abban. The material wasn't solid, but flowed sluggishly, like liquid gold suspended in a viscous material.

The others gasped. Kim looked down.

There, rising out of the depths, was a creature.

Okay, so maybe her first instinct had been to take a step backwards. But she held her ground.

She was here with her friends. And Menefry wouldn't let anything happen to any of them.

Or he'd die trying.

In regards to the first ship they'd been transported in, Kim had agreed with Saxon's assessment, after looking it up. The ship had superficially resembled an Earth-based sperm whale.

Now, she knew that hadn't been the reference point at all.

Instead, that ship resembled the creature who floated in front of her.

It was that dark gray color that Kim would only match with the brightest of pinks, to liven it up some. Its eyes were set far apart on what could only be assumed to be its face. Each one was huge. If she was judging things correctly, if she stood on the bottom eyelid, she might or might not be able to reach the top eyelid. The color was the same gold as the ceiling, with no discernible pupil.

Small appendages dangled just below what could generously be called a face. They waved delicately in the air. Vestigial? Or did they grow and change, like an Oligochuno's arms?

Kim suddenly understood the fluctuation of gravity at the threshold to this place.

While they still had gravity where they were standing on the balcony, the opening before them had none.

"I am Belaitha," the queen said. Her voice was melodious, rich enough to swim in. "What is it you seek?"

Wow. That was one of the queens? Kim hadn't imagined them being this big at all. She'd also assumed that they'd look identical to the rest of Chonchu. But now that she was thinking about it, she realized that she'd never seen a picture of a queen in any of the reference material that she'd been able to dig up.

She could kind of see the resemblance between this queen and the rest of her people: the flat face, the peaked forehead. Belaitha didn't have a nose, or a mouth, not really. Merely sort of a slit.

But some serious evolutionary changes had had to have occurred for her to be the leader of the hive mind. What did the queens look like as children?

"We seek help for our companions, the three beings who make up the secondary engines of the ship *Eleanor*," Judit said, stepping forward.

"Not for yourselves?" Belaitha asked.

Huh. The queen wasn't speaking through that slit that Kim assumed was a mouth. No, the words were coming out of the speakers hanging on the walls nearby.

"While we are also under scrutiny from the Cartel, we can deal with our own problems ourselves," Judit said proudly. "It's our friends who need your help. We did all we could, but their issues needed more expertise than we had."

"The amount of honesty you express is refreshing," Belaitha said. Her vestigial limbs waved slightly.

Was that amusement Kim heard in her voice? It was difficult to tell. But the Chonchu, like the Khanvassa, expressed emotion using their hands instead of facial expressions. So maybe the queen's hands were laughing, or at least smiling.

Judit tilted her head from side to side, a way of producing a shrug for those beings who didn't really have shoulders. "I don't have much else to offer," she said.

"Why do you consider the pod your friend?" Belaitha asked.

Before Judit could answer, Kim spoke up. "Eleanor is like a sister, you know?" she said. "Your highness," she hurried to add. "I can talk with her. Would take her out on a job if she could leave the ship. She's just...good people. You know?" Kim knew that she was repeating herself. It wasn't that she was nervous. Just maybe, perhaps, a little awed at talking to someone who was So. Damned. Big.

"I concur," Judit said. "I've often thought that I'd like to take Eleanor out for a drink some night, just the pair of us, talking shit about everyone else."

Kim frowned at Judit, though she doubted that the captain could see her expression in the dark. Really, even Kim knew enough not to swear in front of royalty.

"Eleanor once mentioned the *Jaimeng*, asking us to join her pod," Judit said. "So that she wouldn't feel so lonely."

The queen bobbed slightly in the air for a moment. Was she surprised? That was what Kim would guess. As well as possibly nodding her head.

Saxon spoke up. "Abban and Gawain have spoken with me about grief," he said in his most stuffy manner.

Kim nodded approvingly. He would be the most formal speaker among them.

"We've also spoken of the afterlife, of your beliefs of a

soul made up of pieces that eventually find their way to become part of a queen's soul," he added.

"Gawain and I have spoken of ways to keep the ship safe," Menefry said. "Though he is more concerned with the engines, he still wanted me to expend my expertise to our travel through hyperspace."

Though Kim didn't stare at Basil, she knew zie should speak up next. And zie didn't disappoint.

"Eleanor is my friend," Basil said softly. "I work closely with her, and I have tried to bring joy into her life, to make her laugh."

Kim couldn't help but smile at that. She remembered how hard Basil had worked at becoming a pirate for Eleanor, figuring out how to wear a black eye patch on zir sensing ring, as well as forming the rest of zir body into a sort of peg leg.

"You speak of the pod as individuals, which had been our hope at the start of the program, to develop a level of independence, while still remaining, at the heart, as Chonchu," Belaitha said. "However, the loneliness of being apart from us has caused them issues. They are bathing in our presence currently, reluctant to continue."

Kim couldn't help but feel crushed by that. She'd hoped that the three Chonchu would want to remain as part of the crew, would want to continue exploring the galaxy with them.

It wasn't because she just wanted to steal the ship and sell it to the highest bidder. No, she'd have to find the exact *right* person who wanted *Eleanor*, and who would treat the three Chonchu as friends.

That might have taken her forever, but it would have been a worthy search. And they could have had all these fun adventures in the meanwhile.

"I see," Judit said, though Kim could tell that she was also sad. Mainly, she just sounded tired.

"Could we at least say goodbye?" Kim asked before Judit could.

"They may yet still join you," Belaitha said. "Give them time to heal. In the meanwhile, I invite you to travel to Eptil, our home world. Very few outsiders have ever seen it. I believe that visiting with us will bring you additional understanding of your crewmates. And possibly you'll be able to meet one of their adjacent pods, those who were closest to yours."

"Thank you," Judit said.

Hey, she even added a slight bow! Awesome!

"As for your ship, we will wait and see what we can do to help you after that," Belaitha said. "Oh, and do not worry about The Universal Trading Cartel. They cannot sense your presence inside the ship that met you, and they will not be able to trace you on the surface of the home world."

"Thank you," Judit said again.

Even Kim breathed a bit easier at that.

"The Chonchu can speak directly to me, or any of the queens, at any given time," Belaitha added. "If you have a message for me, merely tell one of them. The only way I can speak to you is like this."

"How exactly does that work?" Basil finally spoke up. "How you keep in contact with the Chonchu?"

Again, Belaitha made that kind of weird bobbing.

Was the queen laughing at the question?

"We all have our own secrets," Belaitha finally replied. "And this is one of ours."

Kim could tell that Basil was a bit disappointed in that answer. Maybe she'd have to pair up with him, see if they could steal that bit of information. However, she was afraid it wouldn't be written down anywhere, and there wouldn't really be the opportunity to do any sort of experimenting on the Chonchu.

She'd have to find something else to steal, that might cheer up Basil and the others.

It would certainly cheer her up, particularly if there was no more *Eleanor*.

CHAPTER 7
FREDRICK

Fᴀᴇᴅʀɪᴄᴋ sᴀᴛ ʙᴀᴄᴋ ɪɴ ʜɪs ᴄʜᴀɪʀ ɪɴ ʜɪs ᴛɪɴʏ ᴏғғɪᴄᴇ and looked up at the ceiling, trying to figure out what was rubbing his fur the wrong way. The monitors that covered the walls of the office were showing various streams of data: times and dates of spaceships coming and going throughout the system and the various hypergates; market prices of some of the consumables supposedly linked to economic health; search results of banking transfers between two fictitious companies, as well as others.

It wasn't a proper "data bath" as Fredrick called it, with all the various streams color-coded and flowing across his white fur. It was still comforting to have all that information at the tips of his claws.

Today, Fredrick wore one of his usual vests, a soft green in color, complementary to Universal blue. Though what he wore looked simple, it was actually incredibly sophisticated in terms of the hidden cooling units, designed to keep a Yu'udir from overheating.

He'd just received a message from Thyme, the Oligochuno manager he'd met with on the *Niocia* space station, who'd talked with him about Riley, the Bantel who'd taken her own life rather than come and work for him.

Though Fredrick had known that he shouldn't feel guilty at Riley's suicide, he still had. One of the ways he'd assuaged that guilt had been by speaking with Manager Thyme.

At first, Fredrick had kept the correspondence along professional lines, sending official condolences, followed by more personal ones. Appeared that Riley wasn't still in touch with her nest family, so there weren't really any relatives that he could have spoken with.

He had found it surprisingly easy to talk with the Oligochuno. Maybe because they had both started off on the same footing, with a deep and abiding respect for Universal.

However, Thyme had once made a slight slip, and had expressed a concern about how things were being done by upper management.

Instead of disparaging zim, Fredrick had encouraged such thoughts by sharing some of his own misgivings.

They'd started a regular correspondence that Fredrick had enjoyed. Not that he was tired of Clayton—the pissant little Human who was his boss—and was looking for a more cosmopolitan point of view. Thyme was as small town as it got. But zie at least had an appreciation for the big picture, beyond zir own personal gain.

Something which Clayton would never understand. While that supposed cowboy might claim that he had "the good of the herd" at heart, they were still all merely cattle, with him the boss.

The message that had disturbed Fredrick that morning had been from Thyme, letting Fredrick know that zie had a family emergency and would be gone for a short while.

Fredrick re-read the missive for the third time, still trying to pinpoint what had got caught up in his fur about it. It wasn't that he was upset that Thyme was taking some time away. Far from it. Though the manager had never overtly expressed zir growing issues with Universal, he could still read between the lines well enough to recognize that there was some serious resentment going on.

Was that it? Was Fredrick afraid that Thyme, who honestly had become something of a friend, would never return?

That was part of it. There was a finality to the message that the Oligochuno had sent to him. Though zie had merely said that zie wasn't certain when zie would return, the phrasing had felt...off.

Fredrick dug further into the note.

Strange.

Normally, all of the messages that Thyme sent to Fredrick had originated from the *Niocia* space station.

This one appeared to come from a random system, one that was merely numbered and didn't have a name.

Fredrick had dug into Thyme's background when he'd arranged that first meeting with the Oligochuno. He hadn't found anything unusual, that had put up any red flags.

It didn't take him long to find the tiny system that Thyme had sent the message from. It was clear on the other side of the universe, as it were. No planets were close to the hypergates. Once a ship exited hyperspace, they were in for a long run of at least three to four months before they'd get anywhere.

Fredrick brought back up the information he'd originally gathered about Thyme.

Supposedly, zie had been born on the *Niocia* space station. If zie truly had a family emergency, zie should have stayed there, not traveled off into the hinterlands.

Something was off. Something that ruffled Fredrick's fur all the wrong way, that brought his hackles up.

And it wasn't just Clayton, this time.

Fredrick started a few new searches through the databases, looking for more information about Thyme, then immediately turned his attention away, back to the issue that Clayton had brought up, the problem that he was actually being paid to solve.

If there was an actual problem with Thyme, he'd ferret it out.

And put all those niggling fears to rest.

CHAPTER 8

JUDIT

Judit *tried* to be patient. Honestly. She did.

She just found it so frustrating to not be moving under her own power. She'd asked, politely, to at least be given a tour of the ship they were ensconced in, but no one would take her to the main helm. Or the secondary helm. The only place the Chonchu allowed Judit or the rest of her crew to see was the cargo bay where *Eleanor* was currently being held.

Was it just paranoia on their part? After the Chonchu had first been encountered, a plague had taken out most of their queens. Were they scared of history repeating itself?

At least the greeting committee of the Chonchu assured her that it would only be another day before they reached the home world.

In the meanwhile, she and Basil got to "explore" the underside of *Eleanor*, to finally wrench off all of the shield plates and take a really good look at the secondary engine, the one that Abban used for digging through hyperspace tunnels.

Saxon came out to help, and though Judit wouldn't

admit it, she was grateful for his strength when it came to removing some of those damned bolts.

Finally, all the panels were off, and they could see the entirety of the secondary engine.

While the engine itself was possibly only a meter thick, it was at least twenty meters on a side. It appeared to have a center point, that all the tubes impossibly went in and out of. Even though the ship, was powered down for the most part, the tubes still had a soft blue glow to them.

Despite the size of the engine, there was room on all sides for it to "grow." Basil had speculated that the engine itself would expand and contract as necessary for Abban to do zir digging.

Judit wasn't a gearhead. She actually wasn't much of a geek, not as far as she understood the term. She didn't see the point in exposing the entire engine as it was currently in fine working order. Abban would see that when—not if, but *when*—zie decided to come back.

However, Basil was incredibly happy that zie had finally had a chance to see the entire engine, speculating how areas of it were representational of actual physical locations in space.

Judit, on the other hand, speculated that giving Basil this opportunity had perhaps been calculated on her part, something more to tie the Oligochuno to her, in case the ship didn't return to full working order.

She would need a crew with whatever ship she captained next. And she'd like to keep this crew.

No matter what it took.

———

"You have got to be kidding me," Judit said, looking again at the "shuttle" that was supposed to take them from the orbiting ship down to the planet below.

The base of the vehicle (she refused to call it a spaceship) was round, maybe two meters in diameter. There was barely enough room for all five of them to sit. They'd be packed in pretty tightly. It stood on spindly legs on the floor of the cargo space, where *Eleanor* was still parked.

The top of the craft was a tall see-through bubble that hinged, opening so that passengers could climb in and sit.

And that was it.

It looked more like something tourists would rent when day-tripping to a nearby scenic location. Not solid enough to survive reinsertion into a planet's atmosphere.

Where was the helm? Or the pilot? The vehicle had come trundling into the cargo area on its own legs. Were they expecting her to fly this thing down? Or was it fully automated?

Judit trusted that even less.

She looked back at the greeting committee, or now, she supposed, the farewell committee. "You expect us to get down to the planet in that?" she asked, trying to keep herself from shouting.

Given the side-eye that Saxon gave her, she wasn't completely successful.

"It's perfectly safe," the shorter Chonchu in the middle, the "Abban" of the group, assured her. "Belaitha will see to it."

"Will she be flying it?" Judit said, still suspicious. The queen was located somewhere, on what she presumed was a space station dedicated to taking care of such a huge creature.

"Of course!" the Chonchu assured her. "Belaitha controls much of the space traffic in this area."

"I see," Judit said, though she really didn't. Then again,

the Chonchu were a hive mind. They might not have individuals who acted as pilots, but instead, just a pod who interfaced with the queen who directed their ship.

"Belaitha is interested in you reaching our world," the Chonchu said.

Judit could tell that zie was trying to be comforting. The queen probably could have had them killed at any point. Judit and her crew were fully in her control, something that still didn't sit well with Judit.

Chances were, if the queen wanted them dead, she would have done it quietly, not arranged for them to streak across the sky in a fiery ball. Unless she really wanted to send that sort of message to…someone. Who, exactly, Judit didn't know. Particularly since the queens tried to keep all foreign influences to a minimum, which included paying larger fines to have a smaller Cartel presence on the planet.

"Fine," Judit said, keeping her juicier, not-fit-for-royalty comments to herself.

Before she strolled over to that death trap, she did turn back to the Chonchu. "Thank you for hosting us," she said stiffly. Though the greeting committee hadn't done much, hadn't even hung out with them, it was better to be polite to them.

They still had *Eleanor* in their care.

The Chonchu looked puzzled for a moment before replying, "You are welcome. All of you. We hope that we will have the chance to meet with you again."

Judit didn't add that they would. Each of them only carried an overnight bag. Most of their belongings were still in the ship.

Even if she never flew *Eleanor* again, she planned on coming back at least once to say goodbye.

Kim had already strapped herself into the smallest chair, bouncing with excitement. "This is going to be so awesome!"

Judit tried not to roll her eyes. Seriously, the Bantel was just too much some of the time.

Most of the time.

Gingerly, Judit found the chair that was best suited for a Human and strapped herself in. Given the padding, or rather, lack of it, she assumed the ride was supposed to be smooth.

There was a kneeling chair for the Khanvassa, and Saxon had a chair that matched hers, just grown twice as big. For Basil, thoughtful straps had been bolted to the floor that zie slid under easily.

The top came over and reattached itself without a thunk or even a click.

Judit wished there were a checklist she could run over. Some panels she could read. Hell, even a dial that assured her that pressure had been achieved inside the vehicle and there weren't any leaks.

Then the far wall of the cargo ship opened, and the vehicle trundled off into the darkness.

At first, Judit tried to tell herself that she didn't mind the ship. They hadn't died yet. The pressure appeared to be holding up fine. They'd lost gravity as soon as they'd left the carrier ship, and she was grateful for the full straps holding her in.

The one neat thing that she really did enjoy was being able to see out in every direction. For once, a craft had enough windows to suit her. (She still refused to call this thing they were risking their lives in a spaceship. Barely an escape pod.)

The planet spread out beneath them. They were too close to see the entire ball, just the rounded edges on either horizon. Most of the world was covered in water, with a small percentage being land. That made sense, given that the Chonchu had evolved from an aquatic species.

Were the queens their "whales"? That was the primary comparison that Judit and the others had come up with. The scale was about right as well.

Were the queens and the Chonchu even the same species? Or were they two species who had evolved side-by-side on the planet, a symbiotic relationship, with the queens directing the others?

The planet drew inexorably closer. There really wasn't a sense of speed, not unless Judit looked to the side and tracked the stars there.

She heard Menefry mumbling, knowing that he was consigning his fate to the hands of the Goddess.

Judit controlled her own fate, thank you very much.

Except now, when they were in the hands of one of the Chonchu queens.

Who hopefully knew what she was doing as they fell, faster and faster, toward the planet below.

CHAPTER 9

KIM

Unlike Judit and Basil, Kim had grown up on a planet. They didn't bother her.

The fact that this one was so danged *quiet* did.

All the vehicles were electric, so they just kind of swished by in the street they walked next to. There weren't any sports cars, or even sedans, just ugly, utilitarian minivans driving past them, all of the occupants plastered to the window and gawking at them. (She learned later that like the spaceships, all the cars were self-driving. Hardly even worth stealing. You plugged in a destination and it just took you there. No fun side-trips or racing around taking curves as fast as you could. Not that she'd ever been that much of a thrill seeker. No, really!)

Kim couldn't hear the sounds of industry, as it were, no humming generators or squawking vendors as they walked down the wide boulevard. The crisp spring air did carry the sounds of birds, with the occasional flock flying above them, dark bodies darting across the pale orangish sky. Trees that resembled what Humans called a palm tree sprouted up in squares cut into the concrete, with rough purple bark and large pale yellow fronds waving over their heads.

What was so creepy was how silent the Chonchu were, the few beings that they encountered as they followed their guide to the cultural center that had been created for foreigners.

Kim knew that the Chonchu could live together in a pod with as few as three people in it. The beings they saw out on the sidewalk were always a dozen or more walking together, moving as a unit, their steps in a strict march, their arms waving in unison.

Silent.

Also kind of creepy.

The sidewalk was wide, probably to accommodate such large pods. The Chonchu who walked past them also stared at them.

It would be *so* hard to blend in here!

Not that there was anything worth stealing. The hotel they'd been set up in was extremely basic. There were eight rooms in their assigned quarters, all the doors facing into a common area. The five of them each had their own room, and their pod guides—a group of four Chonchu—stayed in the sixth.

There wasn't any art on the walls, though they had been painted with a white paint that had a slight opalescent glow to it. The lights were bright and harsh, as were all the lights of the Chonchu. Basil even complained that the carpet was cheap and scratchy to walk across.

Everything was utilitarian. That was the word that kept coming back to Kim to describe the Chonchu. Nothing extravagant or luxurious.

There didn't appear to be a rich side of town. Nor a "wrong side of the tracks" place either.

Everyone was equal, in a way Kim had once read about

in an assigned philosophy class. No one lived like this. No one who could live independent of their neighbors.

Their guides had given them a brief history of the Chonchu people the night before, how the queens had originally fought each other over the precious few resources that the land offered, how the greatest queen of them all (Zenaida) had united the warring kingdoms into a peaceful land with the harmonious people they now saw today.

Only a brief mention was made of the Great Plague that had wiped out most of the queens over a hundred years before. Many of the pods had gone mad in their isolation, without constant contact of the minds of the queens.

Kim nodded at that, figuring that was why Eleanor and the other had had to come back here.

Well, the ship could just make regular trips back here if that was what her crewmates needed.

She was just going to have to find *something* to entertain herself with in the meanwhile.

Kim had asked about the garments that the Chonchu wore, and was happy to learn that their guides would take her to one of the fabric printing machines so that she, too, could have some of the cloth. (SCORE!)

The Chonchu didn't really wear clothing, per se. What they had really was just a piece of fabric that was clipped here and there to hold it together. They also didn't have sexual organs to hide. It was more custom than modesty to cover themselves.

The building the guides were taking them to that day looked like all the other buildings they'd been walking by— big, square, and imposing—as well as three stories tall. Unlike the space station holding the queen, these ugly things were made up of harsh straight angles. The concrete was the same gray as the others, though there were a few taller windows in the place they were walking up to.

Inside, the floor was at least interesting, made out of a cold, hard stone that was brown with golden flecks in it. There were no guards, or any place to buy a ticket. Seemed as though this place was open and free to the public.

The entrance hall was two stories tall, empty and echoing. At least the lights were slightly dimmer in here. Kim always expected everywhere to have a faint fishy smell, but this place carried the scent of dust and staleness, as if none of the windows had been opened in years.

Kim practically skipped over to the first piece she saw on the wall. Art!

She kept a happy smile on her face, even when she saw that it wasn't. It was merely a photograph of the first of the Cartel to land on Eptil.

Still…a covert glance around told her that there wasn't any security, at least none that she could see. No force field protected the hanging piece itself from someone just walking up to it and touching it.

As they were the only foreigners in the area, chances were she couldn't get away with stealing it. Everyone would suspect her immediately.

Still, she considered how she might acquire such a piece as their pod guides started droning on and on about more of the history of the Chonchu.

Kim thought she saw her opportunity when they passed a door that was labeled in Common as a restroom.

"I have an idea," Kim whispered to Judit, just to get an alarmed glare. Then Kim cheerfully added, "I'll be right back!"

"We'll wait for you," one of the guides said.

"No, no, don't bother," Kim said. "I'll catch up."

She threw a pleading glance at Judit, who gave her a puzzled look but then decided to play along. For now.

Giving her enough rope to hang herself?

"What can you tell me about the industry of the southern continent?" Judit said, walking past the guides and continuing into the next room of the cultural museum. "What sorts of goods might they produce that we could trade?"

This caught the attention of the guides and Kim slipped into the bathroom. She didn't actually use the facilities—they were mostly set up for Humans and while she could use them, it was awkward. Her plumbing was different. All she did was wait for exactly two minutes before slipping out the door.

Judit was still keeping the attention of the main guide on her, so Kim could walk back to the first room.

She didn't know what she needed out here. Maybe some time alone? It was awesome to have a crew she could rely on, but she'd been a solo operator for such a long time. Plus, being alone in her room back at the hotel didn't count. The walls were paper thin, and Kim would swear it was Saxon who'd kept her up all night snoring, though he denied it.

Kim was reaching for the photo commemorating the first of the Cartel coming down to the planet, still not sure what she had planned, when a sound made her stop.

Turning around, she saw the door to the museum had opened and a pod had come in.

But this wasn't a pod of adults. She could tell that at a glance. No, they were younger. Not kids, but perhaps teens. They were all shorter than the other Chonchu she'd met, closer to her height of one-hundred fifty centimeters. Their faces were less defined, flatter, and their eyes were more recessed. They also moved less like a unit than the adults, four at the side of the dozen or so swinging their arms carefree.

There weren't any guides with them. Or any adults.

The pod came to an abrupt halt when they saw her.

Kim waved at them. "Hi!" she chirped.

They all froze. Their eyes immediately took on a faraway look. What were they doing? Consulting with an adult? Or with each other?

Interesting! Out of the group, two stepped forward.

"Hello," one said. She had a nasally voice that sounded similar to Abban, but it was also higher, like Eleanor's. "What are you doing here?"

"We're visiting!" Kim said. "Me and my friends," she added with a casual wave toward the other room.

"Your people don't come here," the one at the front said.

The others in the groups swayed slightly, as if a current Kim couldn't feel had just brushed past them.

Kim couldn't help but snort. "What's there to see here in this city?" she asked. "Something rad."

The two at the front looked at each other again. "I don't think there's anything rad to see here," one of them admitted after a moment. "Except you."

Kim preened. She was styling pretty hard that day. Maybe in reaction to all the gray and brown, she'd picked a blouse that had an ombre effect, going from bright orange at the shoulder to dark red along the hem. Her shorts were super cute as well, a lime green. She looked like a flower! To top it off, she'd colored her scales a bright yellow, kind of to indicate the sun, while her eyes were dark black.

One of the others stepped forward, coming to stand next to the front pair. "Is it true that you can change your skin color?"

Their companions kind of glared at the newcomer. What, they weren't supposed to act separate from the group?

Kim decided to encourage what little delinquency she saw.

"It is!" Kim said. "Here, watch." She held out her hand,

then slid the color from yellow, to green, to blue, then back again.

"Pretty rad, huh?" she asked.

"Yes," most of the pod replied. A few actually said, "Rad," instead, then giggled.

"So what can you do?" Kim asked politely. It was best to know what sorts of special tricks the Chonchu had, particularly if she did come back and steal something.

Or maybe just spray paint graffiti all over the Cartel stuff. And perhaps the buildings outside, to brighten up all the gray.

The two at the front looked at each other, then the group split apart and flowed forward, forming into a circle around Kim.

"This," said one of them.

The pod started a complicated dance. They flowed forward and backwards, weaving their arms and their steps together. They passed by Kim without touching her, though at the same time, they were moving fast enough that she felt the breeze they generated. Their fabric flowed out behind them, seeming to shine more as it fluttered by.

Then they started to move faster. Their arms became a blur. Nobody touched her, despite how quickly they danced.

Just to see what would happen, Kim slowly raised one of her arms up and to the side.

Though she didn't actually hear anything, Kim felt a soft sigh go through the room.

The dancers eagerly changed their steps, flowing around the new obstacle.

Kim started to shift from one foot to the other, slowly bringing her arms up and down, almost waving them, as if she were in water. She wasn't dancing with the pod, not really. She *was* interacting with them, a stranger who they had no other way of connecting to. All the Chonchu could speak together, share their minds.

Not with her, though. So anything she did was unexpected.

Though the Chonchu didn't smile, not like Humans did, she could still feel the joy radiating off this group.

Then one of them accidentally brushed against her. The group as a whole fell back immediately, instantly regrouping into the pod they'd originally presented as, standing in front of her.

"That was awesome!" Kim said enthusiastically. "Why'd you stop?"

One of them responded. "We got too close. We should never touch you. Or allow you to touch us. We need to tell the queen now of our error."

The sadness that enveloped them all made Kim sad as well. "Why?"

As a unit, they all pointed to the photo she'd been contemplating earlier. "We allowed one of them to touch the queens. And then the queens all died," came the solemn commentary.

"I promise you, I don't have any cooties," Kim said, a little perturbed. "I've had all my shots." That was just one of the requirements for joining Arthur's quest. Too many bugs could jump species, and sometimes what was fairly harmless to one species would turn deadly for another. So she'd gotten more immunization boosters than she cared to count at the start of everything. Hadn't had a sniffle once since then, which was pretty cool.

"We have to go," the group announced as one.

They turned as a solid unit and flowed out of the museum.

Kim still wasn't sure what they'd done wrong. Or what she'd done wrong.

It had been amazing, though, to be part of that dance. Even if she'd been on the outside, and could never have joined them fully.

With a sigh, Kim went to find her crewmates.

The Chonchu were just so different.

Could they ever find enough common ground to work together?

CHAPTER 10

CLAYTON

Clayton had planned on taking lunch in his office that day, working at his desk, but the invitation from Rosemary, a fellow board member of Universal, proved irresistible.

He wasn't certain why he felt the need for companionship that morning. It wasn't as if he and Rosemary were best buds or shared that much in common. Zie was an Oligochuno who made it a habit to order the most disgustingly colored food when they ate together.

Still, Clayton respected Rosemary's opinion on business matters. Zie was like a shark when it came to negotiations. If he ever needed a second opinion on a contract before his team of lawyers tore it to pieces, zie was one of the people he'd consult.

Of course, they didn't eat at the corporate cafeteria. That was far too blasé. Pedestrian. Plus, Rosemary always wanted to order something weird, that the cooks might or might not have the ingredients to cook.

Instead, they met in one of the small conference rooms on the *Dallas* space station, where Clayton had his offices.

The table was properly set, with starched white linens and heavy cutlery. No real windows, but a hologram took up one entire wall in the square room, filled with what appeared to be a space view—possibly a live feed—showing various ships departing and landing on the station. The air seemed stale in here, as if the filters hadn't been changed often enough. Clayton took a mental note to send an inquiry about that.

Details mattered. A few crumbs along the foundation of the great edifice could be a sign of general decay that needed to be nipped in the bud.

Rosemary was already "seated" when he arrived, though zie disdained chairs, instead, flatting out the bottom of zir body and leaning back slightly. Zie was drinking something vaguely red and gelatinous that continued to jiggle slightly even after zie placed it on the table. Like the other Oligochuno, zie didn't wear clothes on zir slightly pink and segmented torso. Today, zir body bulged slightly in odd places, whatever zie needed carried in "pockets" that zie had grown inside zieself.

They chatted about different investments that they'd made, bragging subtly about their successes and gossiping about other directors who hadn't done as well.

After they'd finished their meal—Clayton a printed steak, cooked rare, just the way he liked it—they both pushed back from the table and regarded each other for a moment.

"While this has been a delight," Clayton started as Rosemary just sat there looking at him, "I'm sure that you have some other business in mind. Do tell?"

Rosemary bobbed zir head from side to side in the equivalent of a Human shrug. "You have a new assistant, yes?" zie asked. Zir voice was always deeper and richer than Clayton expected.

Now, it was Clayton's turn to shrug. "Fredrick is new, but he's been working with me for a few months now." He paused, counting up the time, surprised to realize that it had almost been a year at that point. "I think you met him at one of the dinner parties." Clayton had made a point of inviting Fredrick to some of the casual get-togethers of the members of the board of Universal had, so he could put faces to names and bring his own impressions of the movers and shakers within the company.

At least, at first. Clayton had "forgotten" to invite Fredrick to the last couple. He didn't have any proof that Fredrick wasn't the faithful data hound he presented himself as, which was why he hadn't fired him. Or worse.

Yet.

Rosemary nodded. "The oh-so-polite Yu'udir?"

"Yes," Clayton said. "What has he done?"

"There were searches being done in the contracts database that set off special flags that I'd set," Rosemary said. "Searches that appeared to originate from your office.

"Huh," was all Clayton had to say. Normally, all his inquires and focus were outward, collecting data from the artifice built around the company, not poking around inside the company itself. He'd never thought to put any sort of watchers on Universal's databases, such as contracts.

Was such a thing necessary? Clayton had always assumed his position was unassailable. He kept tabs on the other board members as a matter of course, not because he was nervous about them.

"I thought so," Rosemary said. Zie gave him the equivalent of a Human grin, an expression that only the Oligochuno who'd dealt a lot with aliens had learned. It still looked forced and unnatural on zir, like a cartoon equivalent drawn across zir slightly pink skin. "Have you ever heard of Woodall, Incorporated?"

"I believe that's a shell company of mine," Clayton said with force casualness. "I'd have to check to be certain."

He was lying, and while he wasn't certain how much Rosemary's sensor array could "see," he did wonder if zie could tell how his heart rate had just spiked.

It was one of the companies that he rarely used. The most recent time, though, had been to pay Sachiko money to destroy *Camelot*.

He'd known that Fredrick had found at least one of the other companies that Clayton had funneled money through. How many had Fredrick found? What scent was the Yu'udir hunting?

"It seemed strange to me that such a company, one that is so rarely engaged, has been the subject of some very delicate queries," Rosemary said. "Almost as if someone was covering their tracks." Zie paused. "You will look into the matter, won't you?"

"I will," Clayton promised. He understood why Rosemary had suggested lunch in person, because such a delicate matter shouldn't be committed to any computer, anywhere.

"Good," Rosemary said. "I also wanted your opinion on this deal I'm negotiating."

Clayton allowed himself to be distracted from zir original question, grappling instead with the intricacies of the merger put before him.

Time enough to pursue his hound later, and see if his leash needed to be shortened dramatically.

CHAPTER 11

MENEFRY

THE ROOM THE CHONCHU HAD ASSIGNED MENEFRY WAS more fit for a Human than a Khanvassa. While the doorways were all tall enough for him, he still had to turn sideways to fit into the freshening unit, the bed was barely wide enough, and there really wasn't any cubby that he could comfortably use for prayers. At least the plain white walls were free from adornment, false images of false gods.

Still, he made do. He kneeled down on the far side of the bed, away from the door, then assumed the most helpless position for one of the Khanvassa, flat on his back.

While Menefry had specifically trained so that he could rapidly get to his feet from such a position, he still felt vulnerable in a way that he was unused to.

Must be because he was on an alien planet, in an alien system, and still no guarantee of how they'd leave, let alone continue.

Menefry tried to clear all that from his mind and concentrate on his prayers to the Goddess Nesnefera. He'd left his statues of the eight-limbed Goddess back on *Eleanor*. He didn't know if they would bring comfort to Eleanor, Gawain, and Abban, who remained behind. Hopefully, the entire crew would be reunited soon.

The statue Menefry kept in his sleeping quarters was the Goddess in Flux, her arms waving all around her, one foot raised as if about to take a step. She was painted the traditional black, with a waft of golden fabric draped over her figure. She was who he focused on today, feeling as though he and his crewmates had come to the apex of their journey, the Goddess's foot raised as high as it would go, and now about to descend.

Which way would she step, her foot finally landing, thereby leading the rest of them?

He finished his prayers with the traditional phrase that roughly translated into Common as, "So be it," though Menefry had also heard it translated as, "That is the truth of the matter."

A quiet voice responded, speaking his dialect of the Khanvassa language, "For now and ever more."

Menefry leaped immediately to his feet, all of his hands reaching for hidden daggers and weapons. (While it was important to be vulnerable when in prayers, only the naïve did so unarmed.)

"Peace be with you, proud warrior," the voice continued.

Menefry didn't see anyone in the small room with him. He stayed where he was, still coiled and ready for violence.

"Who are you? Where are you?" he asked, though the rich tone of the voice had given him a clue.

"I am Candelaria, the queen who is closest to your physical location," she said.

"Ah," Menefry said, straightening back up and putting away his weapons. He bowed his head. "I had thought that the queens wouldn't be able to contact us here?"

"No, that's just Belaitha," Candelaria said. "But she has

given oversight of the travelers to me, at least for the time being."

As this Candelaria appeared to be the closest queen to their location, at least physically, that made a level of sense.

"How are our crewmates?" Menefry asked. "Eleanor, Gawain, and Abban?"

"Healing," Candelaria assured him. "They do not regret their decision to leave our presence, but have been undecided about doing it again."

Menefry nodded. That had been what Belaitha had said. "Is there any way we can talk with them?" Menefry said.

"Not yet," Candelaria said. "We're still hoping they will return to you, soon."

"Good," Menefry said. "What can I do for you?" He was aware that a queen reaching out to talk with any one of them was an honor.

"I would ask you about the prayer you just used," Candelaria said.

"The Goddess in Flux," Menefry said. He described her image, how she appeared to be moving from one state to the other, as were he and the rest of his crewmates.

"How many different positions can the Goddess take?" Candelaria asked.

"As many as a people need for her to be in," Menefry said, trying to sound reasonable. The Goddess could take whatever form was required. Throughout their history, the Goddess had filled many roles.

"Is there a form of the Goddess for people coming together? Maybe just two, or maybe more?"

"I'm sure there is," Menefry said. Was the queen asking this because she wanted their peoples to be closer? "I would imagine that it involved four of her arms reaching out to the various parties, while the others were brought together, palms clasped in prayer."

"Maybe like this?" Candelaria asked.

The door of the unit suddenly had an image projected on it. The Goddess appeared reposed, at peace, while her arms were reaching out as Menefry had suggested.

"Almost," Menefry said, though he was more curious than offended that someone other than a Khanvassa might try to create a statue of the Goddess.

He walked up to the projection, still not sure where the camera was.

Perhaps the door itself held the projection equipment?

He lifted first one hand, then the other of the Goddess's, lowering still others, until the pose was more graceful and represented the image that he had in mind.

While the door was completely flat, Menefry almost felt as though he were working in clay as he moved his three fingers up to slide around the features of the Goddess's face, changing her expression from one of serenity to more concentration. The eyes needed to be closer together, the smile more determined.

Menefry hadn't noted the lack of artwork on this world, not until Kim had mentioned it. Yet, here he was, creating a type of art, while working with one of the queens.

When the image was finally finished, Menefry stepped back and bowed his head slightly to the Goddess, before he looked up and asked, "Is there a reason why you wanted this image of the Goddess? It wasn't just for our group, was it?"

The merry laugh that rang out reminded Menefry so strongly of Eleanor that his heart suddenly ached.

"Don't be so certain," the queen said. "Maybe you are that important, that necessary, both to the Goddess's plans as well as our own."

"May she ever guide your way," Menefry replied automatically.

"And yours," Candelaria said.

Though Menefry couldn't say how he knew that Candelaria was gone, he knew her presence had left and he was alone again.

However, the image of the Goddess that now graced his door remained.

Was it a good sign that the queen had been asking about how to come together as a people? Menefry felt certain that the Chonchu chafed at the restrictions that the Cartel had placed on them, and would like to be able to leave their system more easily.

That was the next problem to solve, after the crew got themselves sorted out.

CHAPTER 12

BASIL

To say that Basil was frustrated with the lack of information that zie was able to access on the planet was an understatement.

As an Oligochuno, zie prided zieself on getting along with most everyone. Zie hadn't exactly volunteered to be a part of Arthur's program—there had been that one hacking job that had gone unexplainedly wrong—but since then he'd been working on the ethical and moral side of the law, if not always the legal side.

Hackers gotta hack, ya know?

It wasn't that the systems down here on Eptil were that good. Zie wouldn't call them laughable. Not exactly. But they hadn't really been much of a challenge. And zie had learned zir lesson on the *Balmor* station, and had checked for hidden, secondary channels.

As far as zie could tell, there just wasn't anything to find.

Where did the Chonchu keep their data? Was it all air-gapped, so that only the queens had access?

Plus, there was no chatter. Kim had mentioned how

quiet the planet had seemed to her. As someone who'd grown up on a space station, Basil hadn't noticed.

Not until zie had started poking around the network and found that it, too, was quiet.

Too quiet.

Zie had understood intellectually that the Chonchu were able to communicate with each other without words. (Telepathy? Some neural net that extended past the physical? Were they all in communication with the queens somehow and that then extended to the rest of them? Zie might be willing to give up the last segment of zir tail to be able to answer those questions definitively.)

However, down here on Eptil, the phenomenon appeared to be planetwide. There was no chatter that he could casually listen in on. No broadcasts either, no vids or even old-fashioned radio.

Very little business appeared to be conducted online. And while Basil remembered Eleanor once mentioning that she enjoyed being in zir presence, how happy she'd been when the secondary engineering room became accessible to zim and the rest of the crew, zie hadn't really thought anything of it.

Now, Basil wondered. Their guides had mentioned going to see live performances later that evening. Zie, like the others, had thought that was quaint.

Or was it? Was that how the Chonchu experienced everything? In person? Did the networks they privately chatted on only work when they were all together?

"What do you seek?" asked a melodious voice while Basil was (metaphorically) bashing zir tail, *again*, against the emptiness of the online community around zim.

It took just a few moments to identify that the voice came from a speaker hidden above the cabinets beside the door of the small room zie was staying in.

"The truth," Basil said after a moment.

"The truth about what?" the voice said.

Though the others probably couldn't tell, Basil knew that the voice was artificially generated. It didn't have the right fluctuations to be natural. It came from a vast selection of phonemes and sounds, so that it appeared to be coming from a living creature directly.

But Basil understood that the queens didn't necessarily ever speak out loud.

"About your people," Basil admitted. "How you communicate. How you live. How do you queens direct the Chonchu. All manner of that."

"Are you a scientist?" the queen asked.

Basil tilted zir head from side to side. Zie didn't know if the queen had an optical pickup in the room but zie assumed so. "I dabble. As an Oligochuno, I understand more about the chemical nature of things than the others. But my primary focus has always been systems, computer systems."

"There is not much for you to find in our databases," the queen said, sounding amused.

"I'm very aware of that," Basil replied, trying not to sound as frustrated as zie felt.

"I am Candelaria," the queen said after a few moments. "I am the queen who is closest physically to your group, so Belaitha has passed your care into my fins."

Interesting. Basil had known that the Chonchu were originally aquatic, and still had phrases that referred to that. Did the queens—who Basil was certain were a different species from the Chonchu—also originate in the great oceans? Given their size, that only made sense.

"How may I help you?" Basil said.

"You know the most about how Eleanor and the others were constructed, yes?" Candelaria asked.

"Masala, the original Oligochuno who worked for

Arthur, knew the most," Basil said. Zie still wanted to raise Masala back up, regrow zim from a single segment, just so that Basil could strangle the scientist. Slowly. "I only know what I've been able to piece together from studying Eleanor and the others."

"You don't approve of what Masala did?" Candelaria said.

Basil sighed. "I believe that Masala must have worked directly with scientists from the Chonchu in order to transform the pod as zie did. That work is fascinating, though with consequences that have yet to be understood. However, the 'leashes' zie put on the ship—deliberately causing it to malfunction regularly—some of those strike me as being both cruel and unnecessary."

Lines of code suddenly started scrolling down Basil's computer screen. The "leashes" that zie had already removed from the original code were highlighted in red.

Interesting. Seemed that zie had missed one. No, two.

Hopefully, zie would have the chance to fix those.

"We don't really have the concept of 'stealing,'" Candelaria said after a moment. "One might have a selfish member of a pod, who tries to accumulate more resources than the other members. But that is generally a phase that youngsters go through. As their bonds within the pod grow, they understand that the only healthy way forward is for the entire pod to succeed, not just an individual. So while we initially also disapproved of the 'leashes' as you call them, in the end, we agreed to them being placed. Was that a mistake?"

Basil tilted zir head from side to side. "The Chonchu require a cooler temperature in order to function. Adding heat when things broke down, without adding additional sensors for Eleanor and the others to be able to sense that heat, I feel was still unnecessary."

"Maybe Masala believed that the pod could still feel the heat in their transformed state," Candelaria said.

"Negative," Basil said. "Zie would have known early on that the pod had very few of those sensors left. Plus, the heat wasn't necessary. It is possible to adjust the nutrients that the pod relies on to remain cool even when something breaks down."

"But that is only something you've determined after much experimentation, correct?" Candelaria said. "Masala might not have gotten to that point in zir experiments."

"True," Basil finally admitted.

Zie still wasn't certain that zie was willing to forgive Masala for the other things zie had done.

After a few moments of silence, Basil had to ask, "How are Eleanor, Gawain, and Abban? Are they recovering?"

"They are," Candelaria said. "We have been in deep discussions about what they need in order to be willing to leave our presence again."

"What do they need?" Basil said. "If we can provide it, we will."

"I do not know if you or the rest of your crew will be willing," Candelaria admitted. "Or how feasible it physically is. My scientists tell me that it may be possible, but your crew would be the first to try it."

Basil sighed. Zie was certain that zie wasn't going to like the answer, but zie still felt compelled to ask.

"What exactly are you talking about?"

"The *Jaimeng*," Candelaria said.

"Where we exchange one pod for another?" Basil asked cautiously.

"Yes. Though you aren't technically in a pod, currently. So we would just focus on the second part of the ritual, where you travel to become part of Eleanor, Gawain, and Abban's pod," Candelaria said.

"What all would that entail?" Basil said, intrigued more than concerned. At least for now.

Candelaria put a chemical signature up on Basil's computer screen. Zie recognized it as part of the chemical structure of zir blood. Fascinated, zie watched the metamorphosis that it went through as pieces were added and subtracted.

It was a type of genetic engineering, though it appeared to be a much more natural process than most of the races used, where they attached things as opposed to manipulating the genes themselves to change.

The end result was a tag, or marker, in zir blood that was truly alien. Separate, yet ubiquitous.

"Will this allow us to communicate as you do?" Basil asked.

"Our scientists don't believe so," Candelaria admitted. "That would require more intrusive changes, possibly adding a specialized organ that appears to be unique to the Chonchu."

"I see," Basil said. So perhaps it was a type of telepathy, made possible by specific evolutionary forces.

Such as the queens breeding the Chonchu for their own purposes? Possibly for centuries before they reached this current form? There had been hints that the Chonchu were ancient.

"However, it will enable the others—Eleanor, Gawain, and Abban—to sense you. We believe that their failing lies in their number. If a larger pod, more than three, had gone through the transformation, perhaps they wouldn't have ended up so lonely. They might, however, still require regular trips to bathe in our presence."

"And without undergoing such changes? If the rest of the crew doesn't agree to this?" Basil asked.

"Then the ship *Eleanor* is no more," Candelaria said. "The pod refuses to leave again, to face the universe on their own."

"Not unless we are with them?" Basil said. "Physically part of them?"

"That is correct," Candelaria said. "I will talk with the others of the crew this afternoon, each separately, then you will need to make a decision as to how close you choose to become."

Basil didn't hear an audible click, but zie could still tell that the channel which the queen had opened was now shut.

The chemical structure was still up on zir screen. Zie started to run theoretical experiments on it, to see what happened as blood cells renewed. Would it be transferable to any offspring? Zie doubted it—that didn't appear to be the nature of change.

Zie remembered, a long time before, of longing to fall into a single gender when zie was mating. Those dreams had faded. Zie felt much more comfortable in zir segments than ever before.

Would zie ever mate again? Would that need ever arise? Would zie be able to "feel" the others of the crew, or at least the Chonchu, sense them as they sensed zim?

It was an entirely new set of "leashes" as it were, though this time, for the crew instead of the ship.

As zie poked at the models zie was running, the realization finally seeped into zir skin that regardless of what the others decided, zie had made zir decision.

For better or for worse, zie was already committed to *Eleanor*, and would be until the last of zir segments failed.

CHAPTER 13

SAXON

Saxon sat on the floor next to the desk in his tiny room and pondered what Candeleria had just told him.

For the longest time, Saxon had hitched his star to Judit. He'd been faithful to her. Possibly to a fault.

Now, he was being given the opportunity to turn away, slightly, from his captain. To instead, be tied to the ship.

Was that what he wanted?

The single chair in the room wasn't sized appropriately for a Yu'udir. That meant he could sit on the floor or on the bed.

He knew that Menefry always laid flat on his back to pray to his Goddess. While that wasn't as much of a vulnerable position for a Yu'udir, Saxon still laid down on the scratchy carpet and looked up, toward the ceiling, as he considered his options.

What did he want?

If he was honest with himself, he wanted to be able to go home, to visit his family. He doubted that Flora would ever forgive him or welcome him back—she was too stubborn and set in her ways to do that—but she hadn't cast him off, either. His nieces and nephews could get to know him, apart from the stories that she told. Then they would get to choose, later, as adults, if they wanted to continue to know him or not.

He wanted to be able to provide for them, as he always had, sending part of his regular salary back to them. It kept him tied there. Even though he was officially dead, and had no legal responsibility anymore.

Did he want another tie? One to the ship? This wasn't a temporary contract with easy loopholes. This was a commitment for life.

A knock on the door disturbed his thoughts. "Come in!" he called, knowing who it would be.

He wasn't disappointed. Judit's voice floated down. "Nice impression of a fur rug you got there."

Saxon snorted but didn't bother moving. First came a sigh, then he heard Judit lying down, perpendicular to him, their feet close but not touching.

"I take it you talked with Candelaria," Saxon said after a few moments of shared silence.

"I did," Judit said. She sighed again. "What do you think?"

"I don't know," Saxon said. "I was just about to ask you the same thing."

"I don't know," Judit said. "On the one hand, I'd like to continue flying *Eleanor*. The controls have all been adjusted just right. She's the most responsive ship I've ever had. I like the crew."

"Really?" Saxon interrupted.

"Yes, really," Judit snapped at him. "All right, even Kim is okay most of the time."

Saxon smiled but kept any commentary to himself.

"I just…I don't know. It feels like signing up for a long run, you know?" Judit finally admitted.

Saxon nodded. Yes, that was it exactly. A short run went from one of the hypergates to a planet in a matter of days, if not hours. A long run took months.

Judit had always been adamant about not signing up for long runs. Saxon understood why. The same crew, the same ship, the same routine day in and day out, would make him a little stir crazy as well. Supposedly, the Yu'udir were better suited for that sort of thing, given the long winters on their home world, where they'd been forced to stay inside.

Other Yu'udir. Saxon had grown used to variety, to change, in part because of Judit. Or maybe he'd always been that way, which was why he'd left his own home world as soon as he'd been able to.

"There's no guarantee that this procedure will work," Saxon pointed out. "Expanding the pod might be insufficient for Eleanor and the others."

"Candelaria did say it would be reversible, though we probably wouldn't notice any difference either way," Judit said. "But it's still experimental."

"Just like the ship," Saxon said.

"I wouldn't have volunteered for Arthur's program," Judit said hotly. "I was forced into it."

"Not even now?" Saxon asked, curious. "Now that you've flown *Eleanor*, gotten to know her capabilities?"

The silence that filled the room after that was telling.

"I do want to keep flying *Eleanor*," Judit admitted after a few moments. "This is just a pretty hefty price. You know?"

"I do," Saxon said. "I also have my doubts. And am not thrilled about continuing to be part of a science experiment."

"But?" Judit prompted. "I hear a big ol' 'but' still hanging out there."

It was Saxon's turn to sigh.

"But, I am also curious about what these changes would mean. How they would feel, if I'd notice them at all," Saxon said. "I also enjoy *Eleanor* and her crew. And I don't want to abandon the pod. It would feel as though I'm jettisoning off of a craft after an explosion, safe and secure in a lifeboat, knowing that some of the crew was still on board."

"I have those same thoughts and feelings," Judit admitted. "Eleanor, Gawain, and Abban are part of *my* crew. And you don't abandon crew."

"So what are you going to do?" Saxon said after another long silence. He gently poked Judit's foot with his own.

"Sign up for the long run," Judit said all in a rush. "And tell myself that it won't be that bad. There will still be different runs, different cargoes, new places to explore. New bars to find, new fights to have."

"One day at a time, eh?" Saxon said, feeling a giddy relief.

Judit had committed. And now, so could he.

"*Egyszerre egy kecske*. One goat at a time," Judit told him. "A saying of my mother's, commenting on the ridiculousness of life."

"Indeed," Saxon said. "Sound advice."

"Pffft," was Judit's reply, blowing what Humans called a raspberry at him.

After Judit had gone, Saxon stayed where he was, on his back on the scratchy carpet, looking up at the textured white ceiling. It had a slight sheen to it, and he could almost place stars against it.

Up and away. That had always been the answer for him. Even if his feet were tied to the earth, to his family, his heart was in the stars.

Becoming part of a spaceship was only a further enhancement of his being. Nothing more, nothing less. The problems, as they came up, could be dealt with.

One goat at a time.

CHAPTER 14

KIM

KIM HAD THE FEELING THAT CANDELARIA HAD NO IDEA how to handle a Bantel's natural enthusiasm. But she had so many questions about the procedure! How would they do it? Would it hurt? What would be her abilities afterward? Would Eleanor and the others now be able to change the color of their amber coating? That would be pretty cool.

Candelaria, though, had no idea of what would happen afterward. "It's experimental," was all that she kept saying. "Never been tried before."

"This is going to be a great thing for Eleanor and the others," Kim gushed. She had made a nest on the bed, asking for extra pillows and blankets. It was all white and off-white and *dull*, so she was rocking the brightest outfit she'd brought, orange and yellow stripes that practically glowed, particularly given the neon blue skin she was sporting.

She sat in her nest while chatting with the queen. She couldn't help but giggle to herself sometimes when she thought about it.

Her, talking with a queen!

Still, Kim had questions.

"Not only Eleanor will be able to track us, though, right?" Kim asked. "All the Chonchu. And the queens as well. Right?"

Huh. This was the first time that the queen had really paused during Kim's barrage of questions.

"Yes," Candelaria said. "In theory."

Kim thought for a moment. "I get it. You don't trust us. I know I wouldn't."

"That isn't it at all," Candelaria said.

Kim was pretty sure the queen was lying. It was kind of hard to tell, as they were just chatting online, as it were. But still.

"Look, I totally get it. The last time you welcomed outsiders to your world, you ended up all plague-y and dead. Putting your marker in us makes sure you know where we are all the time, can track us. So we don't end up doing something sneaky-like, that you wouldn't approve of," Kim told her.

She laid back in her nest and contemplated her arm. Should she brighten up that blue, just a touch? Naw, that just paled it out. Better to leave it more saturated.

"I've heard that you sometimes do *sneaky* things," Candelaria finally commented.

Kim just grinned. "I'm a thief," she said proudly. "I *so* wanted to take Eleanor out some time and just steal stuff with her. I'm sure she'd do great at it!"

"I see," Candelaria said. She sounded puzzled. Then again, she'd kind of sounded that way throughout most of their conversation.

"Or maybe I should take Abban. You know. Team building exercises. Since zie is the one who can sneak in places the best."

"And what would you steal? Hypothetically, if you could?" Candelaria said.

"I don't know," Kim said. "Something from the Cartel. Something that would help free you. Or bring those suckers down. You know?"

"What about putting something into place, instead of removing it?" Candelaria asked.

"Oh, like planting a computer virus? Or a new picture? I did that once," Kim said. She bounced a little, remembering. "I was in my teens. Added a painting to a museum. Printed up the card and everything. No one noticed for like ten days. It was awesome!"

"Or replacing the gate guards?" Candelaria said. "Hypothetically, of course."

"Of course!" Kim said. She thought for a moment. "The guards are all known to each other, so bringing on a new team is harder. I'd probably start with making the existing guards sick, making the Cartel bring in a new team, then replacing them with someone else. That many changes would allow the new guys to slip in and be less noticed."

"Really?" Candelaria said. "I never would have thought of that."

"Sure!" Kim said. "Lots of change. Lots of distraction. If I had the time, I might make a couple of rounds of guards sick. That way, no one would know who was supposed to be there. Who are the guards on the gate for your system?"

"Yu'udir," Candelaria said with obvious distaste. "Not that I dislike them in general. But these have a special contract, specifically laying out the penalties for accepting bribes."

"Huh," Kim said. "You might want to pass those contracts by Saxon. I'm sure he could figure out a loophole or two." While the Yu'udir were the most litigious race, that also meant they had the most grifters.

Who could out-con people better than a lawyer?

"Thank you," Candelaria said. "I'll do that later."

"After the ceremony and you know that you can keep track of us," Kim filled in for her.

"You are very astute," Candelaria said after a few moments.

"Thank you!" Kim beamed. "And you're not stuffy at all. Not how I'd imagined a queen would be."

"Thank you, I think," Candelaria said, bemused. "Do you have any other questions for me?"

"Sure!" Kim said. "What is really going on? Why do you really want us to have this operation? It isn't just for the pod."

Again, that very telling moment of silence.

Kim was the communications expert on the ship for a reason.

After a bit, the queen finally told Kim part of her plan.

And Kim approved.

CHAPTER 15

FREDRICK

FREDRICK SAT IN HIS OFFICE, HIS SCREENS PROJECTING streams of data so that it looped across and over his white fur. Though all of the data was color coded, the streams didn't make him as colorful as a Bantel. Not quite. He wore a somber charcoal gray vest that day, the cooling unit cranked as high as it would go to help Fredrick retain more of his equilibrium.

His tenure under Clayton was coming to an end. Fredrick had poked his nose into too many dark corners. Though he'd tried to cover his tracks, he knew he'd been spotted.

And Clayton had too many secrets to hide to allow Fredrick to continue.

There was still one loose end that Fredrick had yet to tie up.

Manager Thyme.

Or whoever it was that Fredrick had been communicating with since Riley's death. If she had even existed, either.

It had taken some time to tease apart the elaborate con

that had been played on him. He still wasn't sure who the Oligochuno had been who he'd met.

Strange how Manager Thyme had disappeared at exactly the same time that the ghost ship Fredrick had been chasing had gone completely off the radar. He couldn't find it in any system.

Manager Thyme, the real one, hadn't had a family emergency. Fredrick had verified that through other channels, and had found internal recordings of Manager Thyme still plucking away at zir desk in that distracting office of zirs.

Though some of the races complained that it was difficult to tell individuals of other races apart, with the Oligochuno, that really was the case. They looked practically identical. Each being had their own unique chemical signature, which was generally how they identified one another.

However, that was also easy to change or mask. Those sorts of chemicals were illegal, but readily available.

Fredrick had a gut feeling that Manager Thyme, Riley, and the ghost ship were all connected. And he'd learned long ago to trust his gut.

Though he didn't have any proof, he'd give it an eighty percent probability that the ship had been one of Arthur's. Rumors had it that Arthur was planning on establishing a separate cartel, his own independent trading arm. Hence, the experimental spaceships that supposedly went much faster through hyperspace.

Then, buried even deeper, Fredrick had run across hints that Clayton's grandfather had something to do with the plague that had taken out most of the queens of the Chonchu.

Suspicious payments that had been recorded in separate, private accounts.

Accounts that Clayton had foolishly used for his own

suspicious payments. Ones that occurred just before, and immediately after, *Camelot* had been destroyed.

It had taken a tremendous amount of patient digging on Fredrick's part to even find hints of these ongoings. Instead of tapping into the Cartel's computer power, Fredrick had brought his own separate processor online just to winnow out the tidbits he'd extracted. That extra level of separation was probably why he was still there.

But now, what was he going to do with all the data he'd acquired?

He knew Clayton's opinion of him—that he was an adequate hunting dog, but just didn't have that killer instinct. Fredrick also knew that his boss was wrong. He'd always held himself back from the kill as part of a long-term strategy to get ahead in the workplace. To let others take the credit, so that he could position himself better later.

To never appear as a threat until it was far too late.

Now, he wondered. Had he held back so long that it had become part of his nature? To never dive in?

When the first stream of data suddenly disappeared, Fredrick knew his time was up.

He pushed himself forward in his chair. The message was already composed. All he had to do was press *Send*.

When a second data stream vanished, Fredrick made himself move. Reached forward with one short, sharp claw and clicked the button.

Sent the data package to Manager Thyme.

The rest of his data streams went out, one by one, until Fredrick was left sitting in the dark, cold from his vest as well as his actions.

Surprisingly, a message popped up on his screen. Clayton, demanding his immediate presence.

Huh. Fredrick would have assumed that Clayton would have other people do his dirty work.

Or maybe the pissy Human just wanted to flaunt his findings to Fredrick, to belittle his "good dog" one last time.

Clayton was in for a surprise if that was the case.

Fredrick's claws had never been blunted for a reason.

Something that Clayton was about to find out.

CHAPTER 16

MENEFRY

MENEFRY STILL WASN'T CERTAIN ABOUT THE performance that they'd witnessed that evening. He had a cousin who loved acting. Menefry had gone to more than one of his performances, and had heard all about how the crowd could fuel the performance.

This was different.

The Chonchu communicated silently with one another, even outside of their individual pods. So Menefry felt as though he was missing half of what was going on, not because the actors were silent, but because the audience had been.

Plus, while the show had been visually stimulating—the costume designer had obviously been influenced by the Bantel—there hadn't been any music. The dialogue had felt stilted, though that might have been because in their honor, the show had been performed in Common instead of in the native Chonchu language.

The tale had been as old as the hills, from the Warring Queendoms era, as one family of Chonchu tried to overcome another family, and failed tragically.

After the performance, after the audience had left, Menefry and the crew had stayed seated. They had been told that the *Jaimeng* was to occur that evening. They all had given blood and been examined by Chonchu scientists and doctors over the past two weeks.

Now, they were ready for the transformation.

Basil had discussed the process with them in more detail, as zie was the one who understood it best. As far as zie was concerned, the Chonchu scientists weren't starting from scratch. They'd already done most of the work years before, as if this had been part of a different plan that had been abandoned and only recently restarted.

Fortunately, the queens held all the knowledge of the prior experiments, and had been able to easily transfer it over to the current batch of scientists.

From back stage, a group of Chonchu wheeled out a large, long rectangle filled with what looked like water. The glass container was at least ten meters long, between two to three wide, and that same amount tall. It gave off a slight blue glow.

Menefry wasn't certain, but it appeared to be the same color as the secondary engines on *Eleanor*.

"Let's do this," Judit said, standing, then walking to the side of the hall and up the ramp, onto the stage.

The others followed, Menefry in the rear.

Something made him look back.

About thirty people had come back into the theatre, and were filling in the seats they'd just vacated.

Candelaria had explained that these were pods that would be considered adjacent to the pod of Eleanor, Gawain, and Abban. Pods that the three had at one point belonged to, whether that be a birth pod or another family pod.

It was their right to witness the *Jaimeng*, of the crew joining their friends' pod.

The lights on the stage made it impossible to see anyone out in the audience. That was all right. Menefry understood the importance of ceremony, possibly better than any of the others.

At his request, the image that still stood on the inside of his door, that of the Goddess bringing peoples together, now filled the scrim at the back of the stage.

Menefry sang a short prayer to her, a thank you for guiding his steps.

There were last-minute instructions from the scientists, testing the waters yet again, before it was finally time.

Judit went first, of course, as was her right.

She stripped out of the blouse and pants she'd been wearing, displaying a black two-piece bathing suit, similar to the outfit she sometimes wore when doing an intense workout. She was Human, so all her curves and muscles were on display. To Menefry, she looked more naked than a Khanvassa who'd been stripped of their shell.

Yet, at the same time, she still embodied the fierceness of the Goddess as Defender. Not the Goddess at War. There was no one more fierce than a mother or father protecting their brood.

With a strong jump, Judit dove into the container. She swam the length of it with surprisingly graceful strokes.

When had she ever learned to swim? She'd been raised on a space station and hated planets. (It wasn't until much later that he learned that her Hungarian space station had public hot baths and pools.)

Next, it was Saxon's turn. He stripped off his usual vest— this one a comforting shade of green—then stood there for a moment, standing proud in just his fur. Unlike Judit, Saxon seemed more dressed without his usual camouflage, a strong warrior about to conquer whatever foe was foolish enough to challenge him.

He, too, shoved off the edge and swam gracefully to the far side. Menefry assumed he'd learned to do such a thing on his home world.

Kim was next. Though the Bantel didn't have secondary sexual organs like the Humans, she still wore a one-piece bathing suit that covered her entire torso under her clothes. Of course, it was in a shade of pink not found in nature, just this side of eye searing.

Unlike the others, Kim had no idea how to swim. It warmed Menefry's soul how Judit and Saxon stood on either side of the container of water, helping her along. She appeared to be having a blast as she splashed along, giggling madly.

Then, it was Basil. As usual, zie didn't have an outfit on. Zie did retract the two arms that zie had grown earlier, which surprised Menefry. How was zie supposed to get across the water without arms to pull zim?

It appeared that the Oligochuno didn't need them. Instead, zie flattened zir tail into a large paddle. By flapping that in the water, it propelled zim across.

Now, it was Menefry's turn.

The Khanvassa weren't necessarily afraid of water. However, it was a very alien substance for them. They couldn't swim. Their shell would weigh them down. Menefry would drown if he tried.

There had been a lot of negotiations and arrangements made so that Menefry could participate in the ceremony with the others.

He still wasn't certain about this.

But the face of the Goddess shone down on him, her many limbs guiding his path.

And the rest of the crew had all gathered around the starting point of the death-filled water trap, ready to help.

Gingerly, Menefry kneeled down on the platform, then

slowly lowered himself onto his back. He couldn't help but shudder as he felt the water trickling in, under his shell, touching the gossamer wings he kept hidden underneath.

Judit grabbed one of his primary hands. Saxon, another. Basil and Kim took hold of his more delicate, secondary hands.

He didn't sink.

And it wasn't just his faith in the Goddess that kept him from drowning.

His crewmates drew him across the top of the water, floating on his shell as if it were the hull of a boat. The lights hanging from rafters above him filled his vision with their brightness. Though he knew he was just imagining it, he thought he smelled the rich incense that the priests used on altars dedicated to the Goddess.

It wasn't until he reached the far side, his horns tapping gently against the edge of the container, that Menefry knew panic.

How was he supposed to get out? He couldn't pull himself out. If he turned over, he'd drown. And his friends, as much as they were there to help him, were not strong enough to lift him out of the water.

Then the miracle happened. Or at least that was how Menefry referred to it.

The hand of the Goddess scooped him out of the water and gently placed him on the floor.

The Khanvassa didn't cry, not like Humans or Yu'udir. Their eyes didn't have tear ducts.

Their equivalent was an uncontrollable shaking of all their hands.

Menefry, overcome with emotion, couldn't stop shaking for a while as he lay on his back, feeling vulnerable and overcome.

Finally, when he was done, he slowly rolled up to standing, instead of snapping upright, as he'd trained himself to.

"Wait," he told the others.

There was one more thing that needed doing, to bind this crew together.

Slowly, carefully, Menefry separated and lifted apart the halves of his outer shell, revealing the delicate gossamer wings underneath.

With gentle, *gentle* hands, his crewmates stroked the fragile wings, lifting them up and helping them dry.

Menefry thought he might fall apart again after they stepped away. However, instead, he carefully lowered his outer shell, then turned around to face them.

They were all together, now, bound as tightly as if they'd been born in a single shell.

Hopefully, Eleanor, Gawain, and Abban would now feel the same.

CHAPTER 17

JUDIT

Judit wasn't sure exactly what she dreamed of the night after the *Jaimeng* ceremony.

It had been violent. Intense. And certainly gone by morning. She would not remember such things.

As had become their habit, Judit and Saxon met in the common room for breakfast. Generally, no one else joined them, either eating alone or in Kim's case, sleeping.

The Chonchu couldn't stomach caffeine, and had no equivalent of coffee. Judit settled for a spicy tea that had a vague, kinda roasted flavor to it. Plus the cold fish tray that their hosts had left them. Sort of like sushi, with unidentifiable fish, served on a crunchy seaweed noodle instead of rice.

Though Judit had found staying on the Eptil home world fascinating, she was really looking forward to getting back to civilization.

Not something she'd ever say in front of their hosts.

"How are you feeling?" Saxon asked as he came over to where she was sitting, in the corner of the wide-open room.

There were no windows, as the rooms on all sides of the common area took up the outer walls. There was a pretty hologram next to the small table that Judit had tucked herself into. It showed a garden with brilliant greenery and bright flowers, which was okay, matched with a star scene that wasn't logical. She liked the contrast of the two, the vibrant warm greens meeting the cold black sky.

"Good," Judit said. "Weird dreams."

"Same," Saxon said, nodding as he helped himself to some of the tea.

"Develop any superpowers yet?" Judit had to ask.

"Now that you mention it, I did notice something," Saxon said. He paused dramatically.

"And?" Judit said. He had to be teasing her. Right?

"My fur is extra luxurious this morning," Saxon said, preening and stroking his black claws down his arm.

"Asshole," Judit grumbled, huffing. He shouldn't scare her like that, but then again, this was Saxon.

"And you? Feel any different?"

"No," Judit said. She'd spent some time that morning trying to see if she could notice anything off with her senses. Everything felt the same, though.

Though like Saxon, she had noticed that her hair had been extra soft that morning. Whatever had been in that water the night before had certainly nourished it.

The whole going through the water thing had been more ceremonial than scientific. It was how the Chonchu changed pods, at least as far as she understood it. One pod stood on one side of the tank, while the receiving pod stood on the other. The individual who was changing pods swam from one to the other.

By taking that same journey, Judit and the rest of the crew had "joined" with Eleanor and the others, even though they hadn't physically been present. The queens assured them that they "saw" the ceremony, though.

The chemical transformation had been initiated afterward, with each of them receiving a different injection.

Had Kim talked with the scientists to get them to color hers such a neon yellow? While the rest of theirs had been like cloudy water?

Judit wouldn't have put it past her. Kim, for reasons unknown, seemed to have charmed the queen, and so had been allowed to go off on her own a few times, apart from the group, meeting with other pods.

Then again, Judit and Saxon had gone on more than one trip themselves, meeting with merchants and other potential trade partners.

"What is the plan now?" Saxon asked.

"I believe we get to be reunited with the rest of our crew," Judit said. "See if what we've gone through is enough for them."

"Good," Saxon said. "And the Cartel?"

Judit sighed. The queens had given the ship a new identity, working with Basil to make sure that it was airtight. The Cartel shouldn't be able to find them, now.

But that only solved their problem. That didn't solve the bigger issue of the Cartel, how to take them down. How to free the Chonchu, so that they could travel like the other races.

Judit had doubts that many pods would want to leave the home world. However, they should have the choice.

And who knew? Maybe Eleanor and the others would act as an inspiration and so more of the pods would want to travel.

"How do we overthrow the Cartel?" Judit asked seriously. "If we just replace them, the same issues will occur, of bribery and foul play. Power corrupts."

Saxon nodded. "And removing the Cartel? Giving

everyone access to the type of technology that Eleanor, Gawain, and Abban represent?"

Judit sighed. "I hate to say it, but the Cartel does serve a purpose. People can't go off and commit war willy-nilly. I'd like to think that at some point we'd evolve beyond that, but we haven't so far."

"There's still war," Saxon said.

"Yes, and the Cartel makes sure that no one really wins," Judit said. "Everyone ends up poorer. Much poorer. That sort of incentive really does quash most of the opportunistic grabs that people in power would take."

It was Saxon's turn to sigh. "We still need to do something."

"I know," Judit said. "And I'm working on it. Trust me."

There had been something that Kim had said, about how the queens communicated, that had caught Judit's interest.

Only time would tell.

———

JUDIT DIDN'T REALLY WANT TO GET DOWN AND KISS THE floor of the spaceship they'd been "swallowed" by.

No, really. It was dusty and the whole place retained a slightly fishy smell. Besides, what would her crew think?

The impulse passed as she exited the little flyer that had brought them up from the planet. If it wasn't the exact same model as the one they'd used flying down, it came from the same manufacturing plant.

But this time, whoever had been flying the ship had decided that the passengers needed a more "scenic" route up to the waiting spaceship.

That had included a near horizontal take off, barely skimming above the buildings of the city, then out, over the water, dipping down dangerously low.

Then doing *something* to the floor, making it transparent.

Judit still felt seasick. Or something. Watching all that water beneath them.

As well as the long dark shapes that floated under that clear water.

Queens? Teenaged queens? The mass of them had unsettled her.

Finally, though, they were up in a *controlled* environment. No more *weather*. That constant hum that Judit more felt than heard, that told her she was in a working ship again.

Home.

And immediately before her, *was* home.

She'd have to check with Basil, but it appeared to her that *Eleanor* had been cleaned. Spiffed up. Something. There was a shine to her that Judit had never seen before.

There were no Chonchu waiting for them in the huge cargo space. Just the ship, with the cargo door wide open.

Judit looked over and grinned at Saxon.

Honey, I'm home!

Gladly, Judit walked aboard the ship, calling out as she stepped across the threshold, "Eleanor? Gawain? Abban?"

"We're here, captain," Eleanor's rich voice replied.

Huh. Judit hadn't realized before then just how much Eleanor sounded like one of the queens.

Judit led the others through the ship's cargo space, up into the working areas of the ship, and straight to the engine room.

The door to the secondary engine room was wide open.

Judit couldn't help but gasp slightly at the change.

The mishmash of green, gray, and steel-colored cooling pipes that covered the walls had been replaced with tubes of silver. The false ceiling had been removed, showing that it, too, was now crisscrossed with pipes. Basil's plant still hung to one side, obviously alive and healthy. The air retained that chemical algae smell that Judit had come to associate with engineering.

The three amber spars on the dais still stood separate and lumpy. Little lights inside of them were on again, each blinking to its own heartbeat.

"You did it, you really did it!" Eleanor exclaimed as Judit drew closer.

Judit closed her eyes for a moment, seeing if she could feel, well, anything.

She kept her disappointment to herself and instead, pasted a smile on her face as she walked forward. "Yes, of course we did," she said.

She stroked the smooth, lumpy side of the tallest pillar, the one she'd always associated with Eleanor.

Was that a spark there? No. Judit must be imagining it.

Eleanor was speaking with the others, as were Gawain and Abban, all greeting their new pod members.

That the three Chonchu could sense them, know that they were really part of the crew, had to be enough.

It didn't matter if Judit couldn't sense them in the same way.

She had her ship back. Her crew.

Now, it was time to finally see if they could make a difference.

Bring down the Cartel.

And hopefully, replace it with something better.

CHAPTER 18

CLAYTON

Clayton sat behind his desk, waiting for Fredrick to arrive.

He'd been a *bad* dog.

Time to thwack his nose. Hard.

Fredrick had gone too far for Clayton to try to retrain him. However, Fredrick had done some good work. This last interview was for Clayton to try to do the right thing, and place Fredrick in the appropriate new job at Universal.

There was also the possibility that an accident needed to befall the Yu'udir. That was just the cost of doing business as far as Clayton was concerned.

Fredrick didn't look subdued as he came into Clayton's office. In fact, he looked unrepentant.

That wasn't good.

"You know why I've called you in here," Clayton said without preamble, after Fredrick had taken his usual chair.

Something else Clayton was going to have to change out, to remove the visitor's chair that was specially designed for a Yu'udir.

"I do," Fredrick said. That was all he said. He appeared to be willing to wait for Clayton to continue.

"You had everything, you know," Clayton couldn't help but point out. "This would have been the ticket that made your career."

Fredrick nodded his head once, acknowledging the fact that he'd just screwed up everything.

"Instead, you chose to throw it all away, continuing to poke into areas of inquiry after you'd already been warned off." Clayton was honestly still a little pissed off at that.

Again, the single nod of the head.

Fredrick knew what he'd done.

"You didn't find anything though," Clayton added smugly.

Fredrick shrugged his shoulders. "You didn't give me enough time," he said, finally speaking.

"Good," Clayton purred, feeling a shark-like smile take over.

The pointed-teeth smile he received in return was unsettling. The Yu'udir tended to not show their teeth when they smiled, particularly to Humans.

What was Fredrick's game?

"There were some fascinating hints, though, of what had occurred," Fredrick added. "Both with your grandfather, as well as yourself. Payments made both before and after catastrophic disasters. Such as the queens in the Chonchu system all coming down with a plague, as well as *Camelot* being destroyed."

Clayton knew that he wasn't giving anything away. He didn't have any sort of physical tell that would alert anyone to the truth.

Still, he would admit that Fredrick's statement made him uncomfortable.

"All lies and conjecture on your part," Clayton said. "You

can't prove anything, particularly since there's nothing to prove."

Fredrick gave him another tooth-filled grin. "As you say. Tracks have been covered well, as if storm winds and snow have filled in the footprints."

Was Fredrick lying? Had he actually found something?

Then again, the main reason Clayton had brought Fredrick on board had been because he'd been able to put together coincidences that a machine wouldn't have noticed: even the smartest of systems couldn't have been trained to follow those scents.

Not like his good hunting dog.

Clayton decided to give him one last chance.

"Do you have anything to report on that last lead you had? The ghost ship we'd been tracking?"

Fredrick considered his response. Was he about to lie?

Finally, he listed off a number. "If I was still hunting, that's the system I would start in," he said.

It took Clayton a moment to bring up the relevant data. "There isn't anything there," he complained.

"Aye," Fredrick said. "The main planets are a long distance from the gates—three to four months away. But that's where I'd start my search. To see if any ship had recently used the hypergate, and where they'd gone from there."

"Universal doesn't keep track of ships leaving the hyper-gates," Clayton told him with a scowl. "Only those entering."

"I know," Fredrick said. "I'd still set watchers on that gate, making sure that I was immediately notified when a ship did decide to leave that space."

As far as Clayton could tell, Fredrick was telling him the truth. "You honestly expect something to be there."

"I do," Fredrick said, nodding. "Call it a gut instinct."

Clayton grimaced. Gut instincts sometimes had a place

in business. Frequently, though, they were merely indigestion from an overly rich meal.

However, Clayton followed his own gut instinct. "You will be working in a similar system," he stated. "Far from the hub of Universal."

That silent nod, accepting his fate, was all that Clayton got as a reaction. No outburst of emotion. Not even resignation. Just agreement.

As Fredrick stood to go, Clayton couldn't help but add, "There really wasn't anything for you to find."

Fredrick turned toward the door, then stopped, and gave that oddly menacing tooth-filled grin to him again. "That is correct. In your systems." Then he turned and jauntily walked out.

Clayton almost called him back. What did he mean, in his systems?

Surely there wasn't any trace outside of his systems?

He couldn't perform any of those searches himself. And he'd just gotten rid of the only person who might have been able find such tracks for him.

He was going to have to have his people contact Sachiko. Again. Though that would be dangerous. There was already too much connection between the pair of them.

He'd trusted that an individual such as herself had a set of completely secure, multi-layered business for dealing with the large streams of cash coming in now and again from the jobs she took.

Everyone he'd asked had assured Clayton that she was discreet and professional.

Had anyone bothered vetting her accounting practices?

With a sigh, Clayton fetched another bottle of his favorite lime sparkling water from the small fridge behind him. He looked out on the holograms that made up the walls of his office, his favorite views of old Earth, the dusty plains and cattle from a simpler time.

After a brief pause, sipping his flavored water, Clayton dove back into action. Time to wrestle this beast to the ground, before it had a chance to make a break for it.

CHAPTER 19

KIM

It was *so exciting* to be back on *Eleanor*!

Plus, you know, full access to her closet again. Though she'd brought some nice tops and pants with her to the planet, they'd been there *forever*. Kim had had to repeat outfits, more than once!

Unlike poor Judit who seemed to have such a mundane collection of colors at her disposal.

For some reason, Judit had never asked Kim for help choosing new outfits.

Strange.

Kim had gotten more than one bolt of the shiny stuff that the Chonchu used for their clothes. It was so pretty, though a little subdued for her tastes. Fortunately, she knew a marvelous seamstress in at least half a dozen different systems, so she could get something whipped up.

Once they left system. Which they weren't about to do for a little bit.

While on the planet, Kim had gotten long strips of the fabric hemmed with a really nice decorative stitch. It had warmed her heart how delighted Eleanor and the others had been with their presents. Kim had even bought some pretty gold and silver clasps that she used to fasten the fabric around the three amber spars in engineering.

Basil never would have thought of such a thing, nor Masala—the Oligochuno didn't even wear clothes, something Kim still had difficulty wrapping her head around. But Kim could tell that the Chonchu really dug their new outfits. It made them more people-like, wearing the fabric that other Chonchu wore.

Not only that, but now, in the meeting the crew was having in the woods room, all three of the Chonchu not only appeared as their regular amber spars in holograms in the center of the table, they also wore the material she'd gifted them with.

Basil was just finishing up zir report about the engines, how everything seemed to be in good working order now. Once the crew had returned to the ship, they had all wanted to run a few tests to make sure that *Eleanor* was in good condition before they left the Chonchu system.

It had surprised the others that as part of the upgrade *Eleanor* now had a more sophisticated weapons system. Menefry had been like a schoolboy in a candy store. The ship couldn't really engage in a battle as their shields were laughable. But being able to threaten more effectively might work out for them.

Particularly with what they'd be doing next.

As the meeting was winding down, Kim stubbornly stuck her hand in the air. It was a good thing that none of the others could tell how nervous she was. She always bopped up and down as she had been, right?

"Yes, Kim?" Judit said in that *oh* isten *give me patience* tone of hers.

"Have we decided where we're going next?" Kim asked brightly.

"That's kind of the purpose of this meeting," Judit said dryly.

"Well, yeah, I know. But sometimes you have a meeting to ask us stuff after you've already decided," Kim pointed out. "What?" she asked, given the pointed looks of the others around the table.

"I take it you have an idea," Saxon said, his voice soothing all the ruffled scales.

"Uhm, yeah," Kim said. "Me and Candelaria. And the other queens."

Interesting. Judit and Saxon exchanged a long look at that. Had the queens also spoken with them?

"So, we all know what the big problem is, right?" Kim asked, looking around the room.

"Beyond your sartorial tastes?" Menefry teased.

"I don't know about you, but I'm *totally* styling these days," Kim said hotly. And she was! Bright yellow top with sequined black stripes, dots, and patches. Why have just one when you could have all three? Her pants matched in reverse, with a black background and these amazing yellow sequins. Her skin was a creamy blue, sure to go with everything!

But Kim refused to be derailed. "The Cartel continues to threaten us and everything," Kim continued.

That sobered everyone.

"The queens and the Chonchu are bottled up here by the Cartel. Though the queens don't believe that a lot of the pods would leave the system, they still want the opportunity. We've seen first-hand that the stories we've been fed about the Chonchu are a bunch of hooey. They're not aggressive. They're peace-loving! They'd just...like a fair shake. You know?"

Everyone around the table nodded. Though their own problems with the Cartel were mostly resolved with the new ship's identity, the fact that there was still a Cartel presented its own difficulties.

"How would y'all feel about booting out the Cartel? At least from this system?" Kim said.

There were other systems. Other plans. But those could wait.

"How?" Judit asked flatly.

"Eleanor?" Kim said. She totally wasn't squirming under Judit's gaze, wanting to spread the blame around.

Eleanor brought up another hologram. It was a long, tall space station, floating beside the three amber spars that made up the Chonchu members of the crew.

"In addition to the experimental spaceships that Arthur created, he also created these space stations," Eleanor continued in her warm voice. "You've already traveled to one of them. It holds Belaitha."

"Interesting," Basil said, zir nasal voice rising in pitch. "Can it move on its own? Like a ship?"

"Yes, it can, but not very far and not very fast," Eleanor assured them. "These space stations were specifically constructed to connect with the crude interfaces that the Cartel has built around the hypergates."

"The queens and I talked a lot about how to circumvent the current station that's attached to the gate here," Kim said. "How we could steal it." She gave the rest of the crew a big grin. "You know I'm a thief, right? The best there is?"

"Right," Saxon said. "So what you're suggesting is that we, what, steal the existing space station that's currently part of the Chonchu hypergate, and replace it with Belaitha's?"

"Exactly!" Kim said.

"How will we even get close?" Menefry said. "All of the

Cartel gate stations are heavily fortified. You can't just destroy it."

"Nope," Kim said with a grin. "We get to be sneaky about it."

CHAPTER 20

SAXON

Saxon did *not* approve of this.

Any of this.

At all.

However.

The Chonchu really had been treated shoddily. And if he had the opportunity to put things to right, well, what sort of a person would he be if he didn't help?

While they'd been planet-side, one of the things that both he and Judit had noticed was the high level of technology that the Chonchu had. It was subtle, but obvious, particularly once you started looking for it. The fully automated cars and ships. The amount of leisure that the average Chonchu took for granted. The quality of their electronics, not just industrial but consumer, such as they were.

What level would they be at if the Cartel hadn't interfered? If they hadn't had to work their way back up to the current levels of sophistication after a biological catastrophe?

Though Judit and Saxon had focused on merchants and trade goods, they'd also spent some time speaking with engineers about their spaceships.

Before the Cartel had arrived, the Chonchu already had interstellar travel. While they'd found the existing hypergates, as predicted by physics, they'd also explored the less-stable gates, and has ways to exploit them. Particularly since those gates allowed for quick, in-system travel.

Say, between a space station located on the far edges of a system and a hypergate at the center of things.

That was the main advantage of the tunnels that someone like Abban could dig, going between planets in a single system quickly.

It meant that no place was actually now a "long run" away from the rest of civilization.

But that had all been speculation on the part of Saxon and Judit.

Until Kim had let them in on the plans that the queens and Arthur had hatched long before.

Or at least some of the plans. Saxon knew that the Bantel was still hiding something behind that obnoxiously orange-colored skin.

No matter.

Though Judit still had issues trusting Kim, Saxon had become much more of a believer. Particularly after meeting with more than one of the queens.

So here he was, on the tiny Cartel space station that was connected to the apparatus surrounding the hypergate tunnel that led to the Chonchu system.

The queens had followed through on Kim's initial plan of incapacitating the crew of this space station. How exactly, Saxon wasn't entirely certain and honestly didn't want to know.

But the crew of Yu'udir who had been assigned to the space station had fallen ill. First one guard. Then a second.

New food was brought in. All new supplies. And yet, something continued to make people sick, two or three falling ill every week. On a space station with hundreds, that wouldn't have been a problem.

When you only had three dozen, it caused issues.

This changed the mix of people dramatically. Instead of being a single crew, where everyone knew everyone else, all assigned together for a three-month stint, people were being shuffled in and out regularly.

Which meant it was much easier for Saxon to be inserted into the flow of personnel by Basil.

Saxon *hated* the scratchy Cartel-blue vest that he had to wear as part of this con. Not only was it uncomfortable and rubbed his fur the wrong way, it was also ill-fitting. Too short for his torso. It kept riding up, so he was continually tugging it down to cover him better.

And while Saxon in principle trusted Kim, he wouldn't go so far as to allow her to alter the vest sufficiently, not without adding some "flair" to it.

Which just wouldn't do.

Saxon had read through the contract that all the Yu'udir on the space station were required to sign as part of their duties in this system. It was as ironclad as any he'd seen. Truly an impressive bit of knot tying. The fees as well as the countersuits that any individual breaking the contract would receive gave it teeth.

Which was why they couldn't rely on subverting anyone living here.

While it was called a space station, it was actually smaller than *Eleanor* in terms of total area. Like most ships, there was a certain amount of redundancy, with two control rooms to manage the gate, twice as many life-pods as station personnel, two food printers (or replicators, as Humans labeled them), and probably twice as much security wrapped around the communications systems as was normal.

There were only two docks where very small ships,

couriers and the like, could attach to the space station. Anyone trying to break in would have to do a spacewalk, with a good chance of being blown to bits, either by the automated systems on the space station or by the security people here.

When there wasn't much to do on a station, people got bored. And antsy. And they either grew lazy, or hyper-vigilant.

The Cartel had made plans for both extremes by having exceedingly well-decked out game rooms, gyms, and kitchens. They also had regular competitions so that its employees wouldn't grow too inward facing.

Which was one of the reasons why it hadn't been too difficult to get Saxon aboard the station. He came in with one of the supply ships from Eptil, and the first the crew really saw of him was in the gym, working out.

They just accepted him after that, even if he never worked a shift in the control room with the others. Everyone assumed that he was working a shift other than theirs.

Saxon had two tasks while on the space station. To load an electronic virus into the main computer system, then trigger the "all hands abandon ship" alarm at the appropriate time, when everyone else was in place.

What could go wrong?

CHAPTER 21

MENEFRY

Menefry had put his foot down, delicately, gently, but deliberately, when it was suggested that Eleanor or one of the queens should pilot their spaceship closer to the hypergate.

Judit was his pilot. The one with all the training. The one who he actually trusted.

While the Goddess was still in flux, things were also in motion. In a good way.

Menefry sat in the secondary helm this time, kneeling on the piloting couch that was made specifically for him, running yet another check on the weapons' system.

"Would you stop doing that?" Kim asked.

She actually sounded grumbly for once.

"You okay?" Menefry asked. Kim was always cheerful. Always. Not that he would ever say anything to someone who was clearly on the Goddess's Path of Joy. No matter how irritating that individual might be now and again.

"I'm fine," Kim said. She flashed a false smile his direction. "Just because you're using me as bait. And the fact that we're going to be getting too close to that station that has all the weapons on it. Our little gun isn't going to be able to shoot it out. You do realize that, right?"

"I do know," Menefry said. "I understand that the gun is just a backup, in case things go really wrong. But I want to be ready, just in case."

Kim nodded, seeming to deflate. "I get it. Me? I would just wing it. But I know that you're not as into improvisation as I am."

"No one is as good at it as you are," Menefry assured her, trying to bring her joy back, help her feet regain her Path.

"You're right," Kim said, her cheery side surfacing again. "That's why I'm here with you. To help you improvise."

"Though nothing's going to go wrong with the plan," Menefry said, trying to bring comfort not only to her but to himself.

"Right," Kim said sarcastically. "Because nothing ever goes wrong with any sort of con."

Menefry tilted his head from side to side. At least he felt as though he was getting better at this sort of misdirection that seemed to be second nature to Judit, who'd come up with the majority of the plan once the pieces had been laid out.

But what plan ever survived contact with the real world?

Still, he felt better that she was in the main helm piloting the ship, even though they were still in hyperspace, which meant that Abban and Gawain were actually in control.

At least until they dug their way out.

It had been a slow trip, or had felt that way. Possibly because of the weight they tugged behind them.

"Emergence in one minute," came the helpful reminder from Eleanor.

That had been another change since the ship had come into Chonchu space. The three Chonchu appeared to be working together more. All of them now talked to the rest of the crew at various times, instead of Abban and Gawain being mostly silent unless they were in hyperspace or had specific questions.

"Are you ready to free the Chonchu?" Menefry asked his partner.

"Yes!" Kim said, bouncing. Then she sat back, looking a lot less exuberant. "Is this a better 'mournful prisoner' expression?"

Menefry glanced over. Kim had somehow made her face seem longer. The color of her scales had paled, so it was now more of a sickly orange-yellow. She'd dug up the outfit that she'd worn on the Gamor station, when she'd been in the custody of the Cartel.

Basil had obfuscated most of those records, but had recently had Saxon add cleaner ones back into the station ahead of them.

"I think you'll do fine," Menefry said. He tugged at the uncomfortable blue Cartel vest that he wore, the one that matched the outfit he'd been wearing at the Gamor station as well.

"So gonna rock this," Kim assured him.

Then Abban announced, "Normal space achieved."

And it was showtime.

———

THE SPACE STATION ASSOCIATED WITH THE HYPERGATE tunnel leading to the Chonchu system was on the starboard side as they exited the tunnel.

Judit made a sharp right to get them aligned with the station and approached it, while Kim opened up communications channels.

"Unidentified ship, why are you approaching?" came through the comm harshly.

"Prisoner delivery," Menefry said in what he hoped was a bored enough voice.

Everything normal here, nothing to see.

There was a serious pause on the other end of the line.

"What do you mean, prisoner delivery?" came a different voice. Evidently, the person manning communications had already tossed the buck aside, letting the issue slide uphill.

"Don't you have my orders already?" Menefry asked. He gave an exasperated sigh. "Just a sec. Let me resend them to you. Here."

Kim nodded and forwarded the packet that Basil had prepared.

It didn't contain a virus or anything else that would send up automated warnings. This end of things was supposed to look one-hundred percent legitimate.

The line hadn't been muted on the other end. Menefry could tell by the loud gasp when the connection had been made between the "prisoner" he currently carried and the one who had been taken from the *Gamor* station.

"Let me see this prisoner," the voice demanded.

Menefry glanced over at Kim, who nodded and slumped in her chair.

Menefry flipped on the video so that the station could now see not only her, but him.

"How did you—where did you acquire this prisoner?" the voice asked suspiciously.

An alarm sounded in the background of the station.

"Just a moment."

The line was muted.

Crap. They were supposed to be focused on *him*, not on whatever else was going on.

"Unidentified ship, what is that behind you?" a new voice suddenly demanded. This one had the same tones as Saxon's, in other words, the emergency had just been bumped up the chain again.

Was this the head of the station who Menefry was now speaking with?

"I don't know what you're talking about," Menefry assured the people at the station.

"There's a huge ship following in your wake, that just came through the hypergate," the station head explained.

"What huge ship?" Menefry said. Damn it! Basil's virus was supposed to hide the queen's space station as it approached. The Cartel's space station systems weren't supposed to be able to see it.

What in the name of the Goddess Cursing Families was he supposed to do now?

"Leave the vicinity immediately," the station head ordered. "Or both you and your shadowy companion are going to get blown to bits."

"I still have no idea what you're talking about," Menefry said, maintaining his part. "I have a prisoner transfer. That's all I care about."

Silence greeted him.

"There's something wrong with your sensors," Menefry said. "My ship doesn't show anything behind me."

"Show me," demanded the voice.

Menefry put up a previously taken recording, that showed the space behind him only holding the hypergate, and nothing else.

"See?" Menefry said.

"I am getting conflicting data," the station head admitted after a brief pause. "Only one of our surveillance systems is showing the anomaly. The others aren't."

"What did I tell you?" Menefry said. "Now, which dock should I connect to? So I can hand over the prisoner?"

Menefry knew that those at the station wanted the bait.

It was specifically why they'd chosen to dangle Kim in front of them, that possibility of recovering the prisoner who'd been taken from the *Gamor* system.

Would they go for it?

"Docking privileges denied," the station head said after a few long moments. "This is restricted space. You need to turn right back around and leave this system."

"But my orders—"

"I don't care. I don't like this. Come any closer and this station will blow your ship apart."

"I need to deliver the prisoner," Menefry insisted through gritted mandibles. Really, they had to stay focused on him. Ignore the space station behind him that they could evidently partially see.

Menefry could tell that the station head's attention had already been refocused.

"Look, you need to let me—" Menefry started.

A bright light blossomed from the side of the station, heading their direction.

Menefry instinctively targeted on it and shot back.

His aim was high, as Judit abruptly dropped *Eleanor* down and away, racing out of the way of the oncoming blast.

Menefry still cheered internally when he saw his shot slam into the space station itself.

It might not have done any good, but it made him feel better.

Then he braced himself for Judit's evasive maneuvers, praying that the Goddess guided her hands and they escaped.

CHAPTER 22

BASIL

Bail cursed quietly, wishing that zie could grow another three sets of hands.

Well, technically, zie could. However, every set of limbs past four had less and less fine motor control.

Zie could turn zieself into a damned centipede if zie truly wished. However, it would be doubtful that zie would be able to propel zieself along with all those limbs. No, it would be much more likely that zie would trip over zir own damned feet and fall. Like last time.

Instead, zie had to make do with the four hands that zie had. However, those were barely adequate for flying the huge space station that housed the queen Belaitha.

Particularly while still trying to hack into the Cartel space station attached to the gate.

The controls for the queen's space station were set up for a pod, that is, many individuals all working in concert. More hands than Basil could grow and use well.

And why didn't zie have a pod here helping zim? That's right. Because Judit had manipulated zim into thinking zie could do it on zir own. One fewer group out of their control while trying to pull off this heist.

Zie considered for a moment cursing in Hungarian. The entire crew had learned a few of her more choice swear words.

Then the Cartel space station started shooting. Both at *Eleanor* as well as the space station that Basil was currently on.

Damn it! Hadn't Saxon run the virus program that Basil had created? Or hadn't it worked?

Fortunately, when Arthur had built the queen's station he'd added adequate shields and defenses into it, copying what he'd done with *Camelot*.

It hadn't been enough to save Arthur in the end. But it sure helped Basil now, though zie did wince every time the space station shuddered, suffering another direct hit.

In the meanwhile, Basil couldn't allow the lightshow on the monitor in front of zim to distract zim from the work at hands.

Namely, flying this damned boat close enough to the existing space station that it could make a difference.

Basil had spent the last week modifying all the controls on the queen's space station so that it would properly interface with the Cartel's hypergate system. Most of what had originally been built had been close enough. It had needed to be updated, though.

Now, here zie was trying desperately to slow down the huge craft before they barreled into the existing space station, thereby tearing it off the gate and wrecking all the existing controls.

Not that Basil couldn't repair them. It would just be better to take over a working system.

In theory, the space station had the power to slow its momentum.

In practice, Basil had never flown, well, anything before. Not really.

Judit would have been much better at this. But Judit had to fly *Eleanor*, up and out of the way of the space station taking pot shots at the ship.

Fortunately, Judit was good enough that most, if not all, of those shots missed.

At least the shot that Menefry had fired hit squarely.

The line that Basil had opened to the Cartel's space station communications suddenly squawked, alarms ringing loudly.

Had Menefry managed a lucky shot? Truly damaging the station? Or had Saxon merely used the distraction of the direct hit to trigger the alarm?

No matter.

Lifepods began shooting out of the station, like dandelion seeds in a stiff wind, blowing in all directions.

Finally! Something going right.

Basil found yet *another* security lock on the systems he was trying to get into. No wonder his virus hadn't worked. He'd counted on some level of paranoia and redundancy in the computer systems on the Cartel's space station.

Not this level.

Bail continued to split his attention, pounding on the keyboard with two hands while steering the space station with the other two, pulling hard on the brakes to get them to slow down.

Or there was going to be a collision.

Shortly.

CHAPTER 23

JUDIT

Basil was *not* going to make it. She'd given him as much instruction as she'd been able to in the too brief amount of time they'd had before all of this had gone down.

A month wouldn't have been enough, and Judit had known it.

She couldn't be in two places at once, though. She couldn't fly both *Eleanor* as well as Belaitha's space station.

And after the Cartel's space station had opened fire on them, she was certain she'd made the right choice. She'd been able to get *Eleanor* out of harm's way. Those idiots over on the Cartel station had merely blasted whatever was in front of them. They hadn't sent smart rockets after her. As soon as she'd broken the lock the rockets had on *Eleanor*, they'd fallen off.

But now, Basil was in danger of just smashing into the Cartel's space station.

And there wasn't anything she could do.

Or was there?

Judit felt time slow down as she considered the situation. She'd felt this before, when everything around her crawled to a one-quarter time while her mind raced, seeing angles, seeing possibilities, seeing *potential*.

Making plans. And contingencies.

Finally, the way presented itself.

Menefry would have claimed that the Path of the Goddess was made clear to her.

And maybe with a bit of luck, Judit would be able to follow it.

The station had stopped shooting. Or at least stopped shooting missiles and weapons at her.

The only thing it was still shooting at this point were lifepods.

Fortunately, the queens would be sending ships up from Eptil to collect all those up, as they didn't have the ability to survive re-entry into an atmosphere.

Judit calculated the angles again in her head. Basil would come close. But zie would still not quite make it.

And a head-on collision between the two space stations was something that they couldn't afford.

Judit drove *Eleanor* back in close to the Cartel space station. Proximity alarms started screaming at her.

Better *Eleanor* take a controlled bit of damage than Belaitha's take an uncontrolled amount.

Judit banged her ship into the Cartel's space station much harder than she'd anticipated. The netting on her pilot's seat held her in place, but she was likely to have some bruises tomorrow.

Price of doing business.

Judit continued to drive *Eleanor* forward. The ship was honestly about the same size as the Cartel's space station. However, *Eleanor's* bulk was taken up with empty cargo space, while the Cartel's was less hollow.

Still, Judit managed to press it back. She could only

imagine the groaning sound the connections to the hypergate mechanism were making as those tore apart.

Hopefully, not all of them.

Then Belaitha's vessel was upon her. She had the magnification of the camera focused on it turned all the way up.

The Belaitha's station gave the Cartel's a glancing blow. It wasn't too hard, there wouldn't be that much damage.

Then it flew past its target, coming to rest completely just beyond.

Good.

Kim's cheery voice called out, "Minimum damage. Way to go!"

"Thanks," Judit said.

It appeared to her that everyone involved in the engagement had suffered no more than a bloody nose. No broken bones or trips to a clinic were necessary.

Now, they just had to swap out the two stations. Before any of those good Cartel workers showed up.

CHAPTER 24

SAXON

Though Saxon had been the one to pull the hull breach alarm on the Cartel's space station, he'd still found his way to a lifepod and left, just so no one would be able to track the action to him.

Plus, Menefry had done some damage to the space station with his lucky hit. Saxon had used that as an excuse to flip the switch, making the alarm more believable.

The lifepods had minimal maneuvering capabilities. However, Saxon had managed to not shoot away with the others, and had remained in the vicinity of the queen's space station.

It hadn't been alarming *at all* to have that giant tentacle suddenly shoot out from the station and grab him, hauling him toward a dark opening in the side. Nope. Hadn't ruffled his fur in the slightest.

Though he hadn't planned on such an event, it appeared that the queen had prepared for the possibility of him coming aboard, and had a smart gray vest in his size waiting for him. It wasn't his usual tweed, though close, as it appeared to be woven partially out of the fabric that the Chonchu favored.

It was a little shiny for his tastes, though he was certain that Kim would have labeled it too stodgy for her.

He was honestly just happy to be out of the damned Cartel blue that he'd had to wear as part of his disguise.

Now, Saxon stood in a viewing room, watching the work being done outside the station by large pods of the Chonchu.

Both Basil and Judit had damaged the couplings joining the Cartel's space station to the gate mechanism. However, under Basil's direction, the Chonchu crew had managed to remove the other station in only three hours.

Saxon had been prepared for a much longer wait while the queen's space station was attached. They'd been planning on days.

Not merely an additional three hours.

As the last of the physical attachments were made, the electronic and computer systems booted up. The pods of Chonchu released themselves and pushed off, floating a short distance from the hinge that connected the station to the gate.

A hum reverberated beneath Saxon's feet. The noise grew louder, more insistent. It felt as though the space station was moving, though the outside view showed that they remained stable.

Then a flash of...*something*...went through the room.

For a split second, Saxon would have sworn that they'd just entered hyperspace.

Then the hum died down, the thrumming returning to the normal background ambiance of an active space station.

Saxon watched with a huge grin as the aperture of the gate opened and closed.

Belaitha was now in control of the hypergate leading to the Chonchu system.

And this was just the beginning.

———

SAXON MET WITH THE OTHERS ON *ELEANOR*, RETURNING to the woods conference room. Though Basil had fiddled some with the holograms projected on the walls, so that red eyes no longer peered through the trees, watching them, it still wasn't Saxon's favorite room. It was too warm, too dank and closed in. Though he could no longer see the eyes, he still felt as though they watched him.

It was good to see everyone again. It had been three days since they'd successfully brought the queen's space station online. Basil had worked continuously, until Judit had forced zim to go sleep for a time. Zir skin still had gray tones to it, but at least had some healthy shades of pink in it now.

Saxon still wasn't certain of the exact extent of the relationship between Kim and the queens. She appeared to be in a "trusted advisor" position, while the rest of them were somewhat at arm's length.

Eleanor, Gawain, and Abban stood as projections in the center of the faux wood table, shiny material draping their amber forms. Kim was correct in her belief that Basil would never have thought of such a thing. She claimed it made the forms more "people-like."

While Saxon might regularly question the Bantel's sartorial choices, he agreed with her that the three Chonchu who made up the secondary engine did appear more "people-like." Less like frozen amber spars and more like statues.

Interesting that Eleanor gave the report about the condition of the queen's space station, and not Basil. Everything appeared to be functioning, though.

Judit had raised the question again of what happened if the Cartel sent a bomb through the gate, not caring if they damaged the gate itself, just as long as they destroyed the queen's space station.

Eleanor's laughter sent a shiver down Saxon's back, raising the hackles across the back of his neck.

"They can try," Eleanor finally said. "We control the hypergate now. We can detect such things and shunt it off to another hypertunnel before it comes through our gate."

Saxon understood why he'd suddenly had such a chill. While it was Eleanor speaking, at the same time, it wasn't.

Belaitha was also there, speaking through the Chonchu.

"How exactly will you do that?" Basil asked, ever the nerdy scientist.

"We control all of the hyperspace tunnels in this sector of space, now," Belaitha finally admitted.

Saxon nodded, remembering that strange flash when it had felt as though the station had briefly entered hyperspace. He suspected, though he didn't know for certain, that the station wasn't merely connected to the hypergate. Instead, it was connected directly to the hyperspace tunnel.

"How many stations did Arthur build? For the queens?" Judit asked.

"One thousand, five hundred and thirty-eight," came the precise number.

Saxon gave a low whistle. That was many, *many* more than he'd been expecting.

"They aren't all located in this system, are they?" Judit said. She sounded angry. Well, angrier than usual.

"No, they are not," Eleanor/Belaitha responded. "They are scattered throughout all the other systems."

"That's enough stations to control about a quarter of the hypergates currently in existence," Basil said.

The silence that greeted zir pronouncement was telling. That was something else that Saxon and the others had been told many times: the queens, and for that matter, the

Chonchu, couldn't really lie. Instead, there were just lies of omission.

"Or possibly all of them, if you can get most of those into place, yes?" Saxon hazarded. "Control all of the hyperspace tunnels?"

"Yes," Eleanor/Belaitha said. "Now that the first one is connected, the rest will be easier to attach."

"Did we just help an alien species take over our entire hypergate system?" Judit said, asking the question that Saxon and the others also had.

"Totally!" Kim replied cheerily.

Saxon was actually pleased that he was not on the receiving end of Judit's glare, though he did have the fur and claws to withstand it.

"I take it you knew about this from the start," Judit growled.

Saxon wasn't certain if he was going to have to physically hold Judit back from leaping across the table and strangling the Bantel. Or if he should.

At least Kim was cognizant of the danger she was suddenly in based on how her entire body just froze up.

"Yes," she said slowly. "But only after I talked with the queens a whole bunch." She sighed. "And they showed me this."

Eleanor brought up a projection. A beach, somewhere down on the planet below them, littered with huge rocks.

No, those rocks were moving. Trembling. Dripping with black ichor.

It took a moment for Saxon to realize what he was seeing.

An entire beach of queens. Dying. The camera panned back, and the devastation became much more obvious. Overwhelmingly so.

He couldn't count the number of bodies he saw dying there. Certainly hundreds. Possibly thousands.

"They were poisoned by the Cartel," Kim said.

Saxon looked at her, curious. He'd never heard that tone before.

It sounded as though Kim was actually angry.

"To show their trust, the queens brought me to the place they'd brought the Cartel, where they'd done such damage," Kim continued.

The location on the projection changed. Suddenly, they were underwater. A pod of Chonchu swam by, guiding a group of huge black blobs, each blob between three to four meters long.

Baby queens.

"The queens need support and protection of the Chonchu when they're first born," Kim continued. "Then, as they get older, they support and protect the Chonchu."

Judit had posited that the two were two species in a symbiotic relationship. That appeared to be the case.

"In order to show their trust, the queens brought me to the birthing lair," Kim said. Her voice sounded soft now, almost in awe of what she'd seen. "They recognized it was their most vulnerable location. It was where the assassin from the Cartel had struck. He'd poisoned the lair. The queens who came to help were poisoned as well. So many died."

The sadness in Kim's voice made Saxon uncomfortable. It wasn't faked, that much he could tell.

Kim sighed. "So," she continued, obviously trying to be more upbeat. "They knew that you'd be hesitant about handing over all of the hyperspace tunnels to them. They gave me the key to destroying them, that I'm passing along to you."

She made a shoving motion with her hands. The computer screen beside Judit came alive. No one else could see the data that flowed over it.

"These coordinates are the lair? Or rather, lairs?" Judit clarified.

"Yes," Kim said. "Along with recipes for more than one poison that would destroy all of them."

Kim shuddered at that. Seemed she didn't like carrying such knowledge around and was happy to relinquish it to Judit.

"All right," Judit said slowly. "So this is a bribe? In order to help them take over, I hold the key to destroying them?"

"Exactly!" Kim said brightly. "Mutually assured destruction."

"They don't have to let me back into their system, once I leave," Judit pointed out. "You said that you could re-route any traffic coming in, right?" she directed the question at the hologram of the three Chonchu.

"True," Eleanor/Belaitha said. "However, while we'd appreciate you keeping this knowledge to yourself, we know that you could also give it to someone else. Anyone. We would have no idea who your assassin was."

Judit nodded, obviously not pleased that she'd been conned into doing this.

Yet, on the other hand, it was a good way of getting rid of the Cartel's control on the hypergate system.

Once they figured out how to attach the other space stations of the queens. That would be a massive undertaking. A simple con wouldn't do it.

"That only gets us halfway there," Judit finally grumbled. "We still need to fully get rid of the Cartel."

"We can't help you with that," Eleanor/Belaitha said. "There's so much of the rest of the universe that we're unaware of. We've been isolated for too long for us to know what to do. However, once you come up with a plan, we will be eager to help."

Judit sighed. Saxon could see the weight of the entire situation had just gathered on her broad shoulders.

"We're all here to help," he reminded his captain softly.

That at least got him a soft smile. "I know," Judit said. "We're just going to have to figure out how, though."

"We will," Saxon said firmly.

After all, they'd already managed to oust the Cartel's control of the Chonchu system.

Taking over the rest of the hypergates was likely to be easier.

As well as getting rid of the Cartel in general.

Right?

CHAPTER 25

SACHIKO

Sachiko ignored yet *another* message from that stupid, over-reaching idiot Clayton.

How dare he question the security of the payments that he made to her? She had adequate levels of shell companies set up. More than adequate to keep her hidden.

Camelot hadn't been her first assassination. Her biggest, certainly.

But she had done the job. Been paid handsomely for it.

Not handsomely enough for her to have to put up with Clayton and his micro-managing.

What the hell had gotten into him?

In the first three months afterward she hadn't heard a peep from him.

She'd actually read the first message. Hadn't bothered to reply to it, particularly given the patronizing tone he'd used. He hadn't accused her of running a loose, easy-to-penetrate operation, but he'd certainly implied it.

Only after the third message along the same lines did Sachiko bother to reach out to her accountant, just to verify that everything was adequately hidden.

As a Yu'udir, he was particularly loyal to her, as well as clever with contracts and banking. His reassurances were enough to mollify her.

At least for a while.

But Clayton continued to harangue her. Sending daily messages at this point.

Sachiko sat in the office area of her little private spaceship and stewed for a while before she decided to check one last time. She'd run all the regular security checks and searches for her stacks of sheltering companies. There wasn't a thread to hold them together that would lead to her.

She was certain of it.

She was safely hidden. Her accountant assured her that her accounts were untraceable.

However, Clayton, for all his assholeness, might also know a thing or two about hiding behind corporate structures.

It was her last day at the *Balmor* station, teaching at the spy school there. It had actually been a delight talking to the best and the brightest students, watching their eyes light up as lightbulbs went off and they put together various pieces of the puzzle that was proper spycraft.

There were two who she'd decided she would keep an eye on. Not because she had some sort of naïve idea of forming her own company and employing them. No, she worked alone and only occasionally hired contractors.

They might become good enough to threaten her, though, if they were ever hired to go after her.

That was the problem with teaching. Students could learn all the instructor's secrets, then replace her.

One of them, the Bantel Char, was not merely good at the physical infiltration side of things, but she had the reputation of being something of a hacker. It wasn't her specialty, but she knew her way around the various computer systems better than most of the students.

Sachiko would bet that Char knew a lot more than any of her other instructors suspected.

If Sachiko sicced Char on ferreting out all the information for one of Sachiko's shell companies, what would the Bantel find out?

Better that Sachiko know, in case she had to hide more efficiently.

It would be a shame if Char was successful. Sachiko wasn't looking forward to killing her.

But that would be the safest route for them all, particularly if Char did eventually live up to her potential.

———

THE SPY SCHOOL ON THE *BALMOR* STATION WAS FUNDED by governments from all the races. Surprisingly enough, most, if not all, of the money actually went toward the school.

Seemed the various governments were sincere about their spies.

However, no matter how modern and up-to-date the majority of the equipment was in the school, they weren't a private, for-hire assassin who had access to more than one fortune.

The room that Sachiko met Char in was rather plain, furnished with a government's sense of design: beige walls, tough carpet that was a particularly ugly shade of brown and nearly indestructible, and plain wooden desks. Uncomfortable, though functional chairs, built for all the various races, were scattered throughout the room.

The computer equipment on the desks, however, was state-of-the-art. Nothing that Sachiko couldn't afford, though she didn't have to skin everything in that faded industrial gray color that "serious" computer nerds preferred.

Char was already in the room working on something when Sachiko arrived. Before the student could say anything, Sachiko held up her empty hand to stop whatever exuberance the Bantel might have spewed.

In her other hand, Sachiko raised what looked like a needle-beam weapon. It was a sleek, dark gray color, and looked like an oblong egg that fit comfortably in the palm of her hand.

A bright red light shot out the one end. Sachiko painted the walls she could get at from the doorway with the device before she stepped into the room, then she painted the wall with the door.

A rippling effect remained behind, a casual lightshow that Char probably couldn't see but that Sachiko could track with her enhanced eyes.

It was the best barrier she could find on the market currently. Using it as she had meant that Sachiko and Char were now in their own electronic cocoon. No extraneous devices could track anything they said or did in here. The hard-wired computers, such as the one Char had been working at, were still connected. But no other device could detect them.

Sachiko had already infiltrated the station's security, such that no one would be able to follow her movements that day.

While those systems were good, she was better.

Sachiko wore her usual teaching attire: full Geisha makeup that subtly altered the bones in her face so that even the most advanced facial recognition wouldn't be able to get a positive match based on her features after she left; a silk kimono in red with a design of fighting black cranes; and her favorite long black wig, the hair done up in a complicated knot, held in place by jeweled sticks that were much more than they seemed.

"Good evening!" Char finally said when Sachiko nodded that the area was finally secure enough for them to talk.

Char was in an eye-bleeding yellow outfit, matched with truly horrendous scarlet red pants. Her skin, at least, was merely a sickly yellow-green, though it did fade to a truly obnoxious blue in places, while her eyes were black-on-black, looking like deep wells.

"Greetings," Sachiko said with a nod. She always tried to present as serene when talking with the students. It wasn't her natural state. She was a woman of action, and frequently appeared energetic in public.

It was merely yet another mask she wore while here.

"I'm glad you could meet me here this evening," Sachiko said, coming over to stand next to where Char was seated.

"Always happy to help someone like you!" Char burbled at her.

"Yes," Sachiko said. "Now, I know that while it isn't your specialty, you have something of a reputation as a hacker."

"I have no idea what you're talking about!" Char said as she gave her a grin. "Really."

"I have a company that I'd like to test you on," Sachiko said. "What sort of information can you find regarding its finances, its parentage, things like that?"

"Oh, a test?" Char asked.

"Something like that," Sachiko said as she handed over the i-stick with all the data.

"All right, I'll get right on that," Char said, already turning back toward her monitor.

Sachiko didn't bother watching the Bantel. Either she'd find something, or she wouldn't.

They agreed on an hour's time.

Sachiko went through the long, slow form of one of the

martial arts she studied, the one with 199 moves that took thirty five minutes to complete.

She had just finished, and was about to go into a second, shorter form, when Char exclaimed, "Got you!"

Sachiko bowed her head slightly for a moment, closing her eyes. What had the Bantel found?

The company hadn't been one of those associated with the *Camelot* job. It should have been completely isolated from everything.

A chill that touched Sachiko's very soul filled her when she came to look over Char's shoulder.

There, laid out in a simple drawing, were most of her shelter companies.

In less than forty minutes, Char had discovered most of Sachiko's holdings. Not all, but a significant chunk of her business.

And she was just a student, whose specialty wasn't computers.

What would a rabid forensic accountant be able to do?

Sachiko didn't want to admit that Clayton had been right to have been concerned about her corporate structure, but he might have been.

Sachiko needed to go fix this. Now.

But first, unfortunately, she had some collateral damage to control. Inflict. Whatever.

"Very good!" Sachiko said as she came up to stand behind the Bantel. "You really passed this test."

Before Char could turn and look at her, Sachiko reached out with her enhanced strength to snap the neck of the Bantel.

She hadn't counted on the Bantel's ability to change the size of their neck ruff.

Most of the Bantel didn't have that ability.

It appeared that Char did.

Instead of wrapping her enhanced hands around vulnerable skin, Sachiko merely had hold of Char's ruff.

Char twisted and drove a hard elbow into Sachiko's side.

Surprised, Sachiko let go.

Char explosively stood up, shoving the chair back at Sachiko as she danced to the side.

"You didn't think I wouldn't come prepared for a test, did you?" Char purred. She still sounded happy, though this was well-laced with smugness. "Not just computer, but physical as well?"

Sachiko narrowed her eyes, studying the student. She made herself appear more relaxed, just a petite woman here, not one enhanced and experienced with killing.

"You're correct," Sachiko said. "This is part of the test."

Before she'd finished speaking, Sachiko *blurred* forward, moving as fast as her enhanced limbs would take her. She stabbed directly for the Bantel's eyes. As they slightly protruded from their face, they were one of the most vulnerable aspects of her opponent and of the race in general.

Of course, Char was aware for that. And had trained to protect her eyes. She somehow not only evaded Sachiko's strike, neatly stepping to the side, she then grabbed hold of Sachiko's arm.

Sachiko knew the move, of course. In an ideal world, Char would pull her past, throwing her off balance.

Ignoring the captured arm, Sachiko kicked out, powerful muscles lifting her leg and driving it forward. She should have connected with Char's knee, freeing herself, possibly dropping her opponent.

How had the Bantel managed to avoid her kick?

Now, Sachiko was in a bad position. Off balance. Her weight not supported. The Bantel putting painful pressure on her wrist, enough to cause someone non-enhanced to possibly fall to their knees.

Char was much, *much* more than she seemed.

Sachiko twisted her hands around, breaking Char's grip and stepping back, regaining her balance.

The Bantel just grinned at her. Then attacked.

Sachiko found her mind divided, one part automatically defending from the flurry of blows, the other part calmly calculating her own opening.

There.

Char had punched forward, her weight and drive perfectly precise.

But she'd made the mistake of focusing on Sachiko's cocked fist down by her waist, anticipating the next blow, not the open palm pushing Char's blow to the side.

In a circular move, Sachiko drove the fist away then swept in. An inelegant knife-hand to the throat. It was the least vulnerable spot of a Bantel because of the ruff. However, Sachiko had the precision and the enhanced strength to make the blow count.

Char staggered back, her hand to her throat, her eyes watering. She made a choking sound, trying to draw breath through a broken windpipe.

"I truly am sorry to have to do this," Sachiko said as she stalked toward the student. "You would have been truly formidable, one of these days."

The Bantel had already dropped to her knees, her mouth gaping. Surprise as well as sadness filled her expression.

It was a strange combination, one that Sachiko hadn't seen frequently.

"Thank you for all that you've done," Sachiko said before stepping behind Char, taking her head in both of her hands, then twisting firmly, snapping the neck.

Sachiko took a few deep breaths.

It was always said that a teacher, at least a good one, learned from her students.

Sachiko had learned much.

Not only were her corporate structures and monetary systems weak, she had fallen into arrogance, believing herself invulnerable. The Great Sachiko, able to destroy space stations all on her own!

When she'd retired, she'd stopped practicing every day. Stopped training as hard as she had been.

She was retired. Surely she deserved a little rest?

Only if she meant to fully retire. Disappear completely. Reinvent herself as someone new who didn't have any of her abilities.

Right now, that didn't matter. She needed to delete Char's work and leave the station before anyone was the wiser.

Sachiko paused as she looked at the damning evidence of the corporate structure still waiting on the computer monitor.

Only forty minutes. Her entire life undone, there for all to see.

Sachiko leaned forward to delete everything.

The screen suddenly went blank.

Then words scrolled up.

Data Delivered

Sachiko stopped cold. What had Char done? Had she sent everything she'd found out to someone else?

A small i-stick pulsed red next to the keyboard. Sachiko picked it up. The small screen was clearly labeled as a heart rate monitor.

With a straight line running across it, not the ups and downs of a Bantel heart.

Had Char set up a dead-man's switch? Believing herself to be at risk?

Sachiko shook her head and sighed. What idiocy had she just committed?

It wasn't the student's fault, but her own, for thinking herself to be such a badass.

Sachiko quickly left the room without a backwards glance.

Was there time for her to disappear completely? Or was she going to have to make the ultimate sacrifice? Go out in a blaze of glory? Ideally before anyone caught up with her?

Only time would tell.

CHAPTER 26

BASIL

PACKETS OF INFORMATION WERE REGULARLY PULSED through the tunnels and gates. It didn't mean that all news was instantaneously available, but major events were broadcast regularly enough that only planets a long run from a hypergate would be behind.

Except to the Chonchu system. The Cartel had stopped all information flowing in and out of there like a dam across a river.

However, with Belaitha in charge of their hypergate, the system was finally connected to everyone else.

Not only could they send out their own news, they could receive it as well.

For the first time in over a month, Basil and the others received all the messages and other news that had been accumulating.

While Basil *could* read everyone's letters as they came in, zie honestly didn't have the time. Sure, zie could have set up a program to scan everything and summarize, but then zie would have to absorb the summaries.

Plus, most of the letters that came in were personal, from

family or friends. No one on the crew was sending coded messages. Not even Kim, though sometimes Basil did have to wonder about the funny, furry bird videos that she preferred.

Really, zie didn't see the point in watching a bird dip its head in water again and again, then splash it all out everywhere, falling over in the process.

Basil had a few colleagues zie communicated with. Reviews of new hardware or encryption services. All under assumed identities, of course.

Plus, zir regular communication with Fredrick.

It didn't surprise Basil when zir computer gave a particular *Ding*, the tone he'd assigned to all messages coming in from Fredrick.

Zie was going to have to let Fredrick know that the family emergency was over and that zie was back. So it took zim a while before zie got around to opening Fredrick's latest letter.

Zie was taking a break in the secondary engine room, waiting for the 3-D printer to generate more wire, when zie remembered Fredrick's letter. Zie rested on the flat of zir tail, opening the letter in one window while still running code and other experiments in the others.

The first line reassured Basil that Fredrick understood about taking time off. However, Fredrick had to warn Basil that this was the last time zie would be able to reach Fredrick at this address.

Fredrick's next words chilled Basil to the core.

> I suspect my boss suspects some level of
> disloyalty from me.

Was that a warning? Was it already too late? Had all of Fredrick's acquaintances drawn the scrutiny of his boss? Of the Cartel?

How much danger was Basil and the crew in? Basil double-checked that zie had bounced the message around a few times before accepting it so that no one could track where it had eventually ended up.

Still. No program was without flaws. A dedicated hacker might have been able to track the Yu'udir's message given enough time and computing power.

Basil wasn't certain what to do next. Zie signed and wiggled a bit, trying to get the segments of zir body to align more comfortably as zie read through the rest of Fredrick's message.

There wasn't much, just the Yu'udir's usual complaint about how tame the food was on the station, how much he'd enjoyed the latest batch of music that Basil had sent him, how Basil shouldn't worry if there were gaps in his communication, that he'd try to find a way to reach out to him again.

Wait. What music?

Basil had never sent the Yu'udir any music. As an Oligochuno, Basil's idea of music was radically different than any of the other races. Zie did *not* understand art that was singularly experienced. Art was meant to be tasted, touched, smelled, listened to as well as seen, all at the same time. Basil never just *saw* anything. Chemical signatures were a part of zir visual spectrum. The Oligochuno experienced multiple layers of data with everything that they "saw" using the orange sensing ring that encircled the tops of their heads.

Toward the bottom of the message was a link to some more "music" that Fredrick thought Basil might enjoy.

Was it a trap? Or an opening?

Basil debated clicking on the link. It could lead to anywhere. Contain anything.

Despite how zir hand floated above the button, zie knew zieself.

The temptation was too great.

Perhaps the Yu'udir understood that as well.

Basil created a safe environment, apart from the rest of the computer systems, before zie clicked on the link.

The data that flowed into zir system was compact. A cube, locked against easy access.

Zie brought it up on zir screen. It really was elegant, with lines flowing into one another. There was obviously a keyhole on one side, something that Basil supposedly already had.

Now, all Basil had to do was to figure out how to open it.

Hopefully, before they all got blown up.

————

It turned out that the keyhole didn't just expect a passcode. The data had been formed to take the appearance of a physical cube, so the keyhole expected exact measurements of the "key" as well as an encrypted code.

Basil spent more than a day combing through all of Fredrick's previous correspondence, looking for a clue, some mention of a device or object, hell, even a key would be nice.

Nothing.

It shamed Basil that Kim was the one who finally made the connection.

Zie tended to take zir meals on zir own in the ship, as nothing zie ate could be shared with the others. Zie knew that some of the Oligochuno added chemicals to their food so that it glowed across all the spectrums of light, claiming that made it more "alive."

The Oligochuno had never been a hunting species, though. Their nutrients came from the land and what they grew, not from flesh. Not to say that zie couldn't defend zieself. Zie had good enough control of zir skin that zie could easily exude poisons, as well as noxious fumes.

Zie was standing at the food 3-D printer (zie still refused

to call it a replicator) waiting for dinner when Kim came bouncing into the shared kitchen.

"Hiya!" she called cheerfully as she made her way to the counter, pulling out containers of various dried leaves, obviously intending to make herself some tea. "Any luck?" she asked.

The crew knew about the cube. Basil had reported it promptly, along with preliminary estimates of its size. Zie had no idea what it contained, however.

"None," Basil said. Zie hadn't meant to sound as disgruntled as zie did.

Zie was just massively frustrated.

"I'm sorry," Kim said. She actually sounded sincere. "Are you sure the key isn't something you already have?"

"I'm certain," Basil said, snapping. "I've run every decryption program I could think of. I even had Eleanor run it past the queens, accessing all of their personal memories. No one has any clue."

"Hmmm," Kim said as she assembled her concoction. Of course, it wasn't just the herbs she added to her drink, but at least half of it was a sweetener that made Basil's sides itch. "Have you tried his i-stick?"

"His what?" Basil asked.

"We copied Fredrick's i-stick. Remember? And those are often used as a key fob," Kim pointed out reasonably, despite how sharp Basil sounded at the time.

"How would that—oh," Basil said after a few moments.

Zie had the exact dimensions of the Yu'udir's i-stick. As i-sticks came in all sizes, there wasn't a standard one. Fredrick's i-stick didn't have precise measurements in centimeters, as Basil recalled. Both its length and diameter contained fractions, adding to the complexity of the key.

Each i-stick had an identity code that could supposedly be used to track its owner, if the person had bothered to set the tracking up. There hadn't been anything special about the code that Basil had seen.

Except that it was, in fact, a code.

"Thank you!" Basil said, hurrying out of the kitchen.

"What about your dinner?" zie heard as zie rushed along the hall.

"You can have it!" zie called back.

"Ewww. Gross."

Basil grinned but kept moving.

Zie finally had a clue.

Now, zie just had to see if it led anywhere.

CHAPTER 27

SAXON

SAXON GATHERED WITH THE OTHERS IN THE ARCTIC conference room aboard *Eleanor*. Basil had cracked the code for the data cube that Fredrick had sent, and zie thought it was important enough that everyone see the results for themselves.

The cool winds off the ice were just in Saxon's imagination, but it still soothed his fur, not ruffled it. The searing blue sky above the white snow was clear, and encouraged him to be more clear-headed as well. Though the others didn't enjoy this conference room as much as he did—both Kim and Menefry were from warmer places—it only seemed appropriate to play the last message from Fredrick in here.

Without much preamble, Basil asked Eleanor to lower the lights as zie brought up the recording that had evidently been at the top of the data stack hidden within the cube, a sort of primitive "Read Me First" file that had to be played before accessing anything else.

At first, all Saxon saw were colored lines of something—numbers, symbols, and words all intermingled in each stream

—looping and playing out across what looked like a white screen.

Then the screen moved, and Saxon realized that he was looking at a Yu'udir. Fredrick, he assumed.

The room behind Fredrick had been darkened so the colored streams running across his fur were highlighted.

Before the Yu'udir could speak, Saxon said, "Pause the recording, please."

Then he turned to Basil. "Do you understand the significance of his appearance?"

Basil tilted zir head from side to side. "The lines of data are from many different sources. The blue one is travel reports from the various hypergates. The red one is some sort of stock ticker, tracking monetary systems. The green one—"

"Not what I meant," Saxon said. "The way his fur is colored."

Saxon wasn't surprised by the blank looks around the table. "This is from one of the oldest poems extant in my, our, culture. The harbinger of the final battles, before the sun is swallowed and endless winter is upon us, appears wearing colored fur. Instead of white, it is covered with many stripes of colors, like a rainbow."

All heads turned from him and back to Fredrick.

"If the king would have listened to the herald proclaiming their fate, his people would have survived. Instead, he went foolishly into battle, setting off the final apocalypse," Saxon said. "I don't know if that is what Fredrick had in mind by appearing as such. But any Yu'udir would know what he represents."

"Any educated Yu'udir," Judit added dryly, "with a taste for lugubrious adolescent poetry."

Saxon nodded, point taken. "Fredrick was far from uneducated," he stated.

Judit had to nod at that.

"Continue playback, please," Saxon said.

The strange lines of data continued to play across Fredrick's fur. It had to have been Saxon's imagination that he could see the fur stirring slightly, as if the colors were accompanied by a soft wind.

The Yu'udir's face looked like his own, though with many more lines of concern around his eyes and not enough laugh lines around his mouth.

"Manager Thyme," Fredrick started off with. "Or whoever you may actually be. I'm assuming that you managed to get a copy of my i-stick, which you used to open this data."

Saxon nodded, waiting as Fredrick paused, his attention caught momentarily by one of the lines of data.

"Station personnel," Basil said softly, interpreting what Fredrick had been looking at. "From the *Dallas* station, where this was presumably recorded."

"I don't have much time left here, I'm afraid. And I didn't have time to assemble this and present you with a *fait accompli*. All I have is raw data. I'm sending it to you as I assume that someone with your resources and, uhm, *talents*, could put this to good use."

The Yu'udir gave a particularly fearsome, tooth-filled grin, showing off all the sharp points.

"I've included a lot of historical data as well," Fredrick said. "I'm hoping that you'll have the time to dig through all of it and put together a more coherent picture of what actually occurred in the past."

Fredrick paused again, looking down. The data streams grew heavier, occluding his white fur, making it glow with streams of color.

It wasn't quite as bright as Kim's current skin color, which happened to be a particularly obnoxious orange that somehow clashed with the blue undertones of the white snow in the conference room.

How soon would the Bantel decide to try this trick, with multiple moving lines of color? From the rapt look on her face, he figured it would only be a day or two at most.

"I know that this single act can't make up for the evil that I've done, or had caused to be done, all in the name of Universal. The Cartel."

Fredrick looked up, his blue eyes blazing. "But I can at least start making amends before I'm cast out into the cold by Aredhros, the god of the dead. It will be many seasons before I'm welcomed into his hall, if ever.

"Thank you again, Manager Thyme, for at least giving me an outlet. I hope that you were actually able to save Riley from her fate. Tell her…Tell her I'm sorry."

Then he said something in Yu'udir. All the others turned to Saxon to translate.

""May the sun shine warm above you and the ice stay firm beneath your feet,'" Saxon replied. "The implication is that he's leaving for battle and doesn't expect to survive it."

"We need to find him," Judit said, turning to Basil.

"Already on it," Basil assured her.

The image of Fredrick dissolved into a thousand streams of colors. They churned together for a few moments before dividing out and cascading down.

File folders appeared. One after another after another. Hundreds—perhaps thousands—of folders, each containing who knew how many additional layers of folders and data?

"Just the top level is damning enough," Basil said. "Primarily bank records. Showing large payments going out through a dozen shell companies to only a few on the other side. It's the timing and dates that are significant."

Zie paused and looked at Saxon.

"The first payment was made two weeks before *Camelot* was destroyed. The second was the day afterward."

Saxon swallowed against a suddenly dry throat.

"This is it. The smoking gun!" Kim exclaimed excitedly.

"It isn't proof," Saxon said, his voice as cold and wintery as a barren ice flow. "It's circumstantial at best. No court would accept it as evidence, particularly since its source is suspect."

"Even if it's the truth?" Menefry asked softly. "Surely that would win out at the end?"

Saxon shrugged. He didn't have a lot of faith in the court system, such as it was. The Cartel controlled most of it anyway.

Though each system tended to have its own local government, in many ways, the Cartel was the only large governing body that the entire universe had.

Basil dismissed the images and the lights came back to full.

The cold walls of snow surrounding them sent a chill into Saxon, instead of comfort, as if he were facing a long winter without adequate supplies.

Judit was looking expectantly at him, so Saxon continued. "There isn't any sort of lawsuit that could be brought against the Cartel. Even if we did manage to find a legal angle that would work, whoever caused the destruction of *Camelot* would be hung out to dry, while the rest of the members of the board would avow no knowledge of the act."

"That actually appears to be true," Basil admitted reluctantly. "All the accounts link to a single individual. The Human who Fredrick was working for, Clayton Slidell. There are other accounts, from the historical records, that are linked to Clayton's mother and grandfather, both of whom appear to be responsible for other cataclysmic events." Zie paused, glancing over at Kim.

"There was some sort of action carried out against the Bantel, done by Clayton's mother," zie said softly. Then zie shifted zir gaze, over to the amber spars in the center of the table. "As well as the poisoning of the queens, financed by his grandfather."

That actually made Saxon feel better, in a way, to know that it wasn't the entire Cartel who'd planned the destruction of an entire race, as well as *Camelot*. Just one individual who needed dealing with.

"That doesn't really solve our issue, though, does it?" Menefry brought up. "If just one person caused all this destruction. The Cartel can wash their hands of him, then continue on as if nothing happened."

Saxon sighed. There was that, of course.

They appeared to be back at square one.

"I have an idea," Judit said slowly.

Saxon couldn't help the smile he felt growing across his face.

His star would rise again. Judit would make sure of it.

CHAPTER 28

JUDIT

Judit had actually been surprised that just a single individual's family could wreck such havoc on the universe.

Then again, there were no consequences. Not really. As long as it was well enough hidden.

"We don't need a court of law," Judit said as the pieces came together for her, the plan aligning brightly in her mind. "Just the court of public opinion."

That brought puzzled looks from everyone. Judit nodded, grateful that they were in this cold conference room, the one that she always felt helped her think more clearly. Her ideas shone as brightly as the blue "sky" above them, reflecting the white snowbanks surrounding them.

She turned to Basil. "You said before that money was all run through a series of shell companies, correct?"

At zir nod, Judit continued.

"Is there any way to at least superficially link other members of the Cartel's board of directors to those companies? I don't expect some sort of deep link, one that would withstand a dedicated inquiry. Just enough so that on the surface, it appeared that most of the Cartel's board was responsible in some way for the destruction of *Camelot*?"

Basil appeared lost in thought. It was interesting how much body language that Judit had learned to read from having such close contact with the Oligochuno. There were no eyes to take a far-away look. Zir orange sensing band around the top of zir head didn't look away.

She could still tell though by how stiff zir body segments got when zie was struck with an idea, how zir head sort of tilted to one side as zie thought.

Basil straightened up again. "Yes. I can do that."

"Next," Judit said, eyeing the rest of her team, "I need names of accountants. Not mild-mannered ones. I want ones associated with criminals, who are zealous at exploiting every nook and cranny when presented with a problem."

"I may know of a few such individuals," Menefry said slowly, nodding.

"Me too!" Kim said happily. "Cousins, kinda."

Saxon and Basil also nodded. Judit had her own list.

"This information can't come out from a single source," she said. "It must be leaked out to the news channels across as many systems as we can hit, all roughly at the same time."

"So what?" Saxon said. He wasn't goading her. Not really. Just impatient for her to explain the rest of her plan. "This Clayton denies it. This really isn't proof."

Judit couldn't help but grin at him. He really didn't see it.

"The Cartel is held together by their charter," Judit said. "One of the many funny things about their charter is their morals clause."

Saxon just rolled his eyes at her.

Like Saxon, Judit didn't think much of the supposed morals of the Cartel. She'd still studied it thoroughly, just to see what was legal and not legal in terms of independent shipping.

"While it doesn't really bother defining legal or moral acts, one of the things that it *clearly* specifies is that whoever is doing it should not get caught," Judit said. "That's really all the board cares about. Even if Clayton denies his actions, the rest of them would probably kick him off the board anyway, and could use the morals clause for their excuse."

Saxon at least looked very intrigued by that.

Judit shrugged. "Not sure if the links that Basil made to the other members would get them eliminated as well. For a while, though, it might be a bloodbath. And in the meantime, while everyone's attention is turned that way, no one will be looking at us."

Before Judit could continue speaking, to tell them of the rest of her plan, Eleanor spoke up. "Or the gates."

"Exactly," Judit said as all the pieces finally fell together.

CHAPTER 29

CLAYTON

Clayton couldn't believe what he was reading.

Of course, the idiots reporting his connection to the destruction of *Camelot* had gotten the details wrong.

For one furious moment, he envisioned himself sending an angry message, detailing just *how wrong* they were, how it had been *all* his idea, his planning, his money. No one else from the board. Just him.

Then he realized the severity of what he was facing.

Someone knew.

Not just a few details. Most of them. Even if the accusations weren't one hundred percent accurate.

There were enough facts there, enough damning connections, that possibly, some smartass lawyer could make the charges stick.

Clayton hurriedly paged through the rest of the news. Maybe he could get the one reporter banned. Or committed, claiming they were paranoid, delusional, and of course, inaccurate.

It wouldn't even be a lie, the last one.

No, here was a report from a different system.

What was the connection between the two? The first one had been a Khanvassa reporter. Now, it was a Bantel. Were they related, somehow? How could the information have gone so fast from one system to another?

Crap. There was a third report, corroborating the first two.

Clayton ignored the call marked *urgent* that had just come to his messaging system. He knew it was from his publicist, wanting to meet to talk about how to spin this.

Or worse, maybe it was one of Universal's publicists. Someone who didn't work directly for him, who would ask some hard questions.

Clayton was just going to deny everything. Of course. He hadn't done anything wrong. Sure, that trail of money might be damning. He'd have to come up with another reason for spending it.

His entire screen lit up with incoming messages.

Somehow, with all his planning and scheming and such, he'd never really envisioned such a scenario.

Well, he wasn't about to fall on his sword like some stupid samurai. Or walk into a shootout with the entire Bolivian Army.

No, he'd find a way to redirect the blame.

Somehow.

———

CLAYTON SAT ALONE IN HIS OFFICE, IMPATIENTLY waiting while the board decided his fate.

The holograms covering the walls showed his favorite scenes of the American West, with empty hills and cattle just off in the distance. A simpler time, when he might have stood as alone as he was now, with only a six-shooter in his hand, ready to face off against the villain.

He continued to deny each and every accusation, of course. Claimed it was all a hatchet job from a disgruntled employee, one who'd conveniently dropped out of all systems.

One minute, Fredrick had been a happy cog in the machinery of Universal, going to work every morning on a distant, isolated system, and the next, he was AWOL with no one having a clue where an almost tw- meter-tall walking fur rug had gotten to.

No matter. At some point Clayton would be vindicated, and he'd have access to his fortune again.

He could send someone after Fredrick at that point.

Clayton almost felt guilty about the others. Though it really had just been him initiating the destruction of *Camelot*, that a dozen other members of the board had also been indicted just proved his claims that all of this "data" was suspect.

He supposed he could have stepped forward and told everyone that the others were innocent. At least, of the crime he'd been accused of. That it had only been him and his genius, his great fortune, that had taken care of the problem that all of them had had.

However, that would have been admitting that he was guilty, and that would never do.

Eventually, it might come out that the others did have clean hands. When that happened, Clayton would also be ready to step back into the limelight and see all the evidence against him destroyed.

He recalled Malina's face as she heard the board call her name as one of those indicted…she would never forgive him. Might even send her own assassins out after him. He'd just have to keep his security doubled, and on high alert.

Since the news had come out, more than one clumsy attack against his life had already been foiled. Seemed a lot of people were angry about *Camelot*. A lot more than Clayton had anticipated, that was for certain.

Wouldn't do for the next attempt, which would be much more professional, to succeed.

There was something that Clayton could do, though. It hadn't been his fault that his involvement had been uncovered. Not really.

It was all the fault of that woman. Sachiko. He'd tried to warn her that her systems were weak.

If they had been impenetrable, the trail wouldn't have been found, leading to him. He was certain of it.

Maybe, he could get everyone's attention focused on her, instead of him? Sure, he may have financed the job (though that was still impossible to prove) but *she'd* been the one to do the deed.

Her hands were much less clean than his.

With glee, Clayton turned his attention to Sachiko. He had all the data at hand. Who should he send it to?

He was about to start the message to his own pet forensic accountants, who would tear through her corporations like the tissue paper they were, when a high priority news alert flashed across the bottom of his screen.

One bearing Sachiko's name.

Damn it! Someone else had already beaten him to the punch.

Some Bantel named Dale had just released all the data about Sachiko and her corporate structure. He had a sob story about how Sachiko had killed the only person he could ever love, even if she'd been a spy.

It was worse than that, though.

This Dale, or whoever he'd hired, had easily found the links between Sachiko's accounts and Clayton's.

Clayton bowed his head and took deep breaths through his mouth as the consequences rolled over him.

The board would see this news and would halt their already damning proceedings, even if they were in the middle of a vote.

The news would spread through the grand chambers, possibly starting as whispers before it became a crescendo of shouts.

He had no chance, now, of anyone believing his innocence.

Not that anyone on the board actually cared about that.

No, Clayton had broken the cardinal rule of Universal.

You could stick your hand in the cookie jar and steal as much as you wanted. Break a few cookies while you were at it.

You could never get caught.

Clayton had for all intents and purposes, finally been caught.

And was going to have to pay the price, no matter how unfair that was.

Crap.

CHAPTER 30

MENEFRY

"But you're asking me to lie," Menefry pointed out to his crewmates. Again.

"No, not outright lie," Saxon assured him. "Just shade the truth. A bit. Mislead them."

Menefry shook his head. He, Saxon, and Basil all sat in the desert conference room, the one that Menefry had taken as his second office. No one else was really comfortable in this room, while it provided a soothing atmosphere for the Khanvassa. He'd even put a statue of the Goddess in the corner, the one in the pose of Sage Counsel, wrapped with a fuchsia colored gauze that Kim had approved of.

All of the team had been recording messages to be sent out to various guards on the stations that were connected to the hypergates in the systems where the queens had stations.

Basil had managed to delay the payment from the Cartel to one such system. All it had taken was a single transposed set of numbers in an account.

Then, all the complaints about the lack of payment had been magnified, with Judit managing to convince more than one news station to play up the news. It was particularly juicy, given that just the day before, half the existing board of directors of the Cartel had been forcefully ejected.

Not from an airlock, unfortunately. But it did mean that the corporation was in some turmoil.

Though Basil had only worked zir magic on one bank, it seems that a second had the same issue that day, so the complaints about lack of payment were abruptly multiplied.

It was the last thing that the Cartel needed.

And it primed all those good workers to be paranoid.

Now, it was up to Judit and the rest of them to prompt those workers into action.

However…

"My word has always been my honor," Menefry explained. Again.

"I know that there are Khanvassa who don't tell the truth," Saxon said, trying to reason with him.

Menefry sighed. "Yes. And no. Perhaps they justify it by only lying to foreigners, and never to their own people. Or maybe they just shade the truth."

"That's all we're asking you to do," Basil said. Zie pushed forward the scripts that zie had written. "All you have to do is follow along."

Menefry shook his head. While Basil had tried to do zir best, there was a reason why Saxon had recorded the messages for the Yu'udir, Kim had done one for the Bantel, and even Judit had done some for Humans. Saxon's had been full of contract law, Kim's had been over-the-top cheery, even for her, Judit's had started with a dirty joke, and Basil's had been all about the nerdy details of the gate.

Menefry's, well, it had to be something even more different for the other Khanvassa.

"Look, you can try it out on us first," Saxon said.

Menefry couldn't help but click his mandibles in frustration at that. "No. I need to talk with some other Khanvassa. Convince them first. Then use that as a script."

Saxon looked at Basil, who tilted zir head from side to side. "We'll use a mostly automated station, at first," zir said. "One that's pretty far out from everything, that only has a maintenance crew, not a permanent one."

"That sounds perfect for a trial run," Menefry said.

He could do this.

It just had to be done his way.

———

MENEFRY SANG OUT HIS GREETING, A BRIEF PRAYER TO the Goddess, wishing luck and benevolence on all who heard his voice.

"Yeah, whatdaya want?" came the reply after a moment.

There was no visual, so Menefry couldn't see the individual he spoke with.

He could practically hear the eyeroll on the other side, though.

Perhaps the individual—Jidimadi was his name—was not as educated as Menefry had originally believed.

"Greetings fellow traveler on the Path of Goodness," Menefry said, still going with the original script he'd prepared.

It was within reason to assume that all beings were on the Path of Goodness, set there by the Goddess. The individual path for someone had to be determined by them, with help from the priests or prayer.

Silence greeted him, instead of the expected greetings.

Hmmm.

"I come to you at this difficult time within the Universal Trading Cartel, to ask for your forbearance," Menefry said.

"As in the tale of the Goddess praying for tolerance, so we, at Universal, are now asking the same."

"What are you talking about, priest?" Jidimadi asked, sounding exasperated.

"Now, you may have heard certain rumors about pay being suspended or even canceled, even for work already done," Menefry said.

"What, you mean like what happened at the Jodpur system? Everyone there got stiffed. Lost more than a month's wages," Jidimadi said.

Menefry sent a questioning look at Basil, bringing up one of his secondary hands to emphasize his confusion.

Basil merely tilted zir head back and forth.

Seemed that zie hadn't heard of it either.

Was the rumor mill taking on a life of its own? As Judit had predicted?

"No, no, I'm not saying that," Menefry reassured the person. "You will be paid. Eventually. I'm sure of it."

"I got bills to pay," Jidimadi warned. "When?"

"I'm not saying that you're not going to be paid. Just that there's a slight chance that it might, perhaps, *maybe* will be delayed," Menefry said.

There. Every word was the truth. There was no reason why Jidimadi wouldn't be paid. Basil hadn't done anything to the banking system in this region.

All that Menefry wanted to do was to put the fear of losing wages into the worker's heart.

"Mealy-mouthed priest," Jidimadi muttered. "Look, can you say for certain that I'll be paid?"

"Of course! Of course!" Menefry said. "I'm just…not certain when. It might be on time. It might…not."

"Fine," Jidimadi said.

"Look, there isn't anything you need to worry about. The Goddess will set your feet on the right path. You don't need to shut down the station at all. Just wait and all will be resolved," Menefry said all in a rush. He added another short prayer, about the Goddess counseling patience.

"Yeah, right," Jidimadi replied. He sang back a verse about the Goddess expecting everyone to do their part.

"Exactly," Menefry said. "Thank you so much for understanding. And all of this will be taken care of as soon as possible."

"I'll just be sitting here waiting," Jidimadi said. "In my shutdown station."

He killed the line before Menefry could say anything else.

Menefry turned to smile beneficently at the other two. He sang out another line of prayer before he pressed all of his palms together and bowed his head.

Yes, the role of the muddled priest come to spread calm was the exact part he needed to play as the news of possible late payments made its way across all the systems.

Hopefully, all the queens would be ready to play their part in the next phase of the game.

CHAPTER 31

SACHIKO

SACHIKO SAT IN HER PRIVATE SHIP, JUST INSIDE OF A hypergate in an extremely quiet system. It wasn't a long run to the main planet. It wasn't a short run, though either—only about two weeks, instead of two months—so the gate wasn't busy and Sachiko could just sit here and think.

She'd set up her own messaging service, so the news was constantly being updated. For a brief time, she thought she'd escaped. Clayton had been exposed by someone, and all eyes had turned to the Cartel. Their illegal exploits had captured everyone's attention.

Then a Bantel, someone who sounded like a grieving lover, came forward with all of the information that Char had found about Sachiko's involvement.

Fortunately, it had all occurred in a short amount of time, so that Sachiko hadn't had to wait weeks before making up her mind about what to do next.

She'd already moved as much money around as she'd dared, knowing that the hounds were nipping at her heels in the electronic sphere. Whatever assets she had remaining had already been seized.

No one would be satisfied, though, until they'd tracked down every credit and found her.

She was going to have to sever the line, hard.

A part of her resented having to amass a fortune again. She'd earned that last one, damn it! And she could never appear as herself again.

The ability to change her face beyond recognition was available to her.

For a price that she could no longer afford to pay.

There were rumors of the Cartel no longer paying its workers, but she didn't see yet how she could exploit those.

Of course, she had fantasies about somehow making it to the *Dallas* space station and taking out Clayton in a blaze of glory. She wasn't worried about him. Someone would see that he had an "accident." She didn't need to clear up that detail herself.

The choices before her remained few. And bleak.

She could make the run to the main planet and stay there. Lose herself forever in this backwards place. Make herself a life, such as it were. She did have assets here, unconnected to any of her other accounts. She wouldn't be broke, but it wouldn't be the life of leisure that she'd envisioned.

She could run to another system. There was yet time. However, most of her safe houses and hidey-holes were currently in the process of being infiltrated.

A warning beep from the console in front of her drew her out of her musings.

She'd parked her spaceship just inside the gate so that she could track any ships coming in after her. So far this past week, there'd only been a single trading ship that had entered the system.

Her system had just warned of another ship approaching.

Strange, though. It hadn't come from the hypergate.

Where the *hell* had that monster come from?

Sachiko shook her head as the ship—no, space station—sailed out of nowhere and slowly came to a halt beside the existing ship that controlled the hypergate.

Fascinated, Sachiko watched as dozens of individuals shot out of the space station and landed on the hinge that connected the Cartel space station to the hypergate.

Could she use this as a bargaining tool? She started recording everything that was happening, how the unidentified people disconnected the Cartel's space station that automatically, remotely controlled the hypergate, then attached the new space station to the gate instead.

As soon as the connections were made, the people all drifted back, small blobs waiting.

A bright, blue-white flash exploded from the newly connected space station.

For a moment, Sachiko would swear that she could *see* the hyperspace tunnel that the gate was connected to. That the new space station was now not just a part of the gate mechanism, but the tunnel itself.

What had just happened?

Was the exposure of Clayton and his misdeeds, along with her own, just a distraction? So that people didn't notice that all the hypergates were being taken over by someone else?

Sachiko had to admit that it was kind of brilliant.

"Watching ship," came the unexpected hail. The voice was warm and rich.

Sachiko froze.

The voice read out not the name her ship was licensed under, but the actual true identification number associated with the engine. It was one of the few ways of distinguishing the real provenance of a ship.

Generally, however, it could only be done by someone physically examining the mechanism.

Not scanned by a space station some distance away.

"Yes?" Sachiko finally replied.

"We are the queens of the Chonchu," the space station announced, still sounding more comforting than it should. "We mean you no harm. We are here to maintain the system of hyperspace tunnels in a manner that is fair and equitable to all."

Sachiko sat back in her chair, stunned.

An alien species had just taken over this gate? She was certain this wasn't the only gate they'd managed to acquire.

"What about the Cartel?" Sachiko asked, merely because she assumed it was expected of her.

"They have been less than equitable about access to the gates," the voice told her. "Bribable. Fallible. We cannot be bribed. And as we are connected to each other across hyperspace, we can work together in a way that the Cartel, no matter how Universal it claimed to be, could not."

Though the voice remained lovely and warm, Sachiko heard her own death sentence in those words.

Once the queens had access to the right databases, they'd know who this ship was registered to.

They'd find her.

Even if she disappeared on the planet nearby, she'd never have a day's rest. They would always be hunting for her. She was good, but as she'd recently proven to herself, she wasn't that good.

She'd make a mistake and they would capture her.

"Thank you for the news," Sachiko said. "I wish you the best of luck."

"And you too, in either your long or short run," the voice said.

It didn't suddenly list out her name, though Sachiko wondered if the space station already knew.

If all of hyperspace was suddenly controlled by beings

who couldn't be bribed, who were interconnected, what would happen to people like her? Would they no longer have access to places and illegal substances? Would crime be limited to backwater areas as every connected system could be so much more easily policed?

What happened when suddenly, crime could no longer pay?

That also wasn't the bright, shiny future that Sachiko wanted any part of.

She turned her ship and took off, plotting a course not for the closest planet, but for the closest star.

Time to go out in a blaze of glory, as it were.

In the meanwhile, Sachiko dismantled all the emergency systems and controls that would stop her ship from immolating itself.

She also flung out data packets as she went. Little chunks of information, almost like breadcrumbs behind her. She could do her bit to clean up the universe, shine a spotlight on all the individuals who'd paid her well to do their dirty work.

Time for them, too, to come clean.

Feeling lighter than she had in ages, Sachiko put on her most formal robes, all in black and red, then sat down to some of the best meals she could prepare given her limited stocks.

While she might have wished for more time, she was surprisingly at peace with her decision.

After all, not everyone was given the choice of when they went. She'd seen to that many times.

It was just her turn, one last assassination before she was done.

CHAPTER 32

KIM

Kim wasn't nervous *at all* about picking up the Yu'udir Fredrick from the hellhole he'd been assigned to.

Nuh-uh.

His rooms were tiny, especially for a Yu'udir. Was that part of his punishment?

The front room barely held enough space for a single Yu'udir-sized chair, a ratty one at that. Definitely a one-butt kitchen, though it appeared as though Fredrick rarely cooked, but ate carryout, based on the containers in his sparse fridge. She'd only poked her nose into the bedroom and hadn't bothered examining it closely, because the entire space was filled with a bed, with only a rack at the end holding endlessly dull Cartel-blue vests.

The crew had decided to scoop Fredrick up before Clayton had a chance to come after him. While Clayton was no longer a member of the board of directors for the Cartel, he still had power.

Maybe not a lot of influence, as it appeared he'd spent much of his personal fortune to kill *Camelot*. And Basil had ensured that the right forensic accountants had been notified of the hidden parts of Clayton's wealth, so everything was being tracked.

Still.

Kim wasn't sure where to wait for Fredrick to come back from his office. They hadn't had time to follow him and scope out his habits. So she'd broken into his (laughably) locked apartment mid-afternoon, ready to wait for him all night, if necessary.

She'd come prepared to disguise herself. It turned out that the Chonchu fabric, though made of cloth, was highly conductive, apparently because it had originated from a type of seaweed. It was the perfect material to apply some of Dale's hiding technology.

So while Kim might appear a bit more subdued than usual in her outfit—the Chonchu fabric wasn't iridescent except under the right lights—she was still styling. Particularly with her oh-so-cool colored striped scales that she'd patterned after Fredrick. He was really going to appreciate that.

She spent a short time finding the perfect place to disappear into—changing her scales to exactly match the wall and cupboard in the front room, her outfit disappearing completely—then she practiced moving her hand across the dark faux wood cabinet, changing her scales from the color of the wall to the color of the wood, staying perfectly hidden even though she was in motion.

It wasn't an easy skill to master, but Kim nailed it. Of course.

Sooner than Kim had been expecting, she heard the front door open. She quickly took her position against the wall, freezing into place and blending in completely.

Fredrick stepped into the front room, not carrying a take-out bag. Maybe he meant to go out again?

He looked around, but didn't see her.

"I know that there's someone here," he said softly. "A silent alarm alerted me at the office. If you're here to kill me, please do so now."

"What?" Kim said. She turned her head so she could better look at him.

The amount he jumped, so very startled by her appearance, was oh-so satisfying!

"I'm not here to kill you," she said as she stepped away from the wall. "I'm here to rescue you."

Kim pushed color into her face, so it was no longer the pasty white of the wall.

That seemed to frighten Fredrick even more.

The black face of the Yu'udir never changed color, either blushing or paling. Instead, the fur around their neck rose, like a ruff. Hackles, Kim seemed to remember them being called.

"Are you…Riley?" Fredrick asked. His fur collapsed in on itself. "You're alive!"

Kim snorted at him. "Of course I am, silly. And my name is Kim."

"Is Manager Thyme with you?" Fredrick asked, looking around the tiny room.

"Nope. Zie's still up on the ship. Waiting for you." Kim took a breath. This was *not* going how she'd planned at all! She pushed on.

"Look, we appreciate what you did. And we figure that Clayton is gunning for you. So we thought that maybe you'd appreciate being moved to someplace else. And we might have a new job for you as well. What do you say?"

Kim realized that she was rushing. Though she was loath to admit it, there was still a part of her that was kind of scared of this Yu'udir.

He would have hunted her, hounded her, through all the systems, if she hadn't faked her own death.

Fredrick blinked, looking stunned.

Okay, so yeah, maybe that was a lot to take in.

"You're not angry with me?" he asked slowly. He moved into the front room and sat down so that he no longer towered over Kim.

"Naw. That happened ages ago," Kim assured him, though in fact it hadn't been that long. Maybe a month or so.

So many things had happened in the meanwhile!

"Good," Fredrick said. "Are you sure you would trust me with a new position?"

His cultured tones reminded her of Saxon when he was about to get pedantic about some point.

Kim just grinned though. "You're right about us questioning your loyalties. I mean, come on, you were the right-hand person for the bad guy. Yes?"

"Yes, I was," Fredrick said. He looked a little puzzled.

Fortunately, Kim was totally used to that expression, since most people, even her crewmates, wore it frequently.

It appeared that not everyone was as straightforward as she was.

Stupid as that was.

You had to be straightforward with people. Particularly your friends. Except when you were being sneaky. That way, you could tell the two apart.

"So we found you a place where you'll be free to do your thing, but kind of be watched at the same time," Kim said.

"All right," Fredrick said though he still seemed wary.

"And the accommodations will be way cooler than this," Kim assured him. She could work with the queens to make that happen.

"You'll be working with the Chonchu," Kim continued on. "Helping their system recover after being isolated for so long."

Fredrick just blinked at that.

Poor guy didn't get it. But the Chonchu needed someone who understood the outside world, and who would work hard to bring them up to date. Who could negotiate all their contracts and help them build new alliances.

Fredrick would fit the bill, particularly if he saw it as penance for all the bad things he'd done in the name of the Cartel.

"Are you ready to go?" Kim asked.

Fredrick looked around the grim little room. A smile of satisfaction crossed his face before he grew perfectly somber again. "Certainly," he said, standing. He risked reaching out a hand to her. "Let's go."

Now, it was Kim's turn to pause. The Yu'udir's nails had never been blunted, and were still sharp claws. His fur was less bright than the last time she'd seen it, less white and poofed out.

He was willing to take a chance. To trust her to lead him to a new future.

She just had to trust that this strange person could also kinda sorta be a new member of her nest.

Fredrick's face had started to fall. Before Fredrick could withdraw his hand, Kim reached out and snagged it. To apologize for her hesitation, Kim abruptly changed the color of her scales, so that lines of color now streamed across it.

The effect wasn't as good as what Fredrick had managed, but she was still working on it.

Fredrick started, then finally smiled.

"I will listen to the harbinger," he said solemnly.

"Good," Kim said, grinning. "Because we got a whole new world to issue in."

And it was all going to be so much fun!

As long as she still got to go steal things once in a while. Just to keep people honest.

CHAPTER 33

MENEFRY

MENEFRY HAD FINISHED HIS PRAYERS, THANKING THE Goddess for her intervention and deliverance these past few weeks.

He still lay on his back in his rooms aboard *Eleanor*. From here, he could just see the statue of the Goddess in Flux above the cupboard, but not much else. There was no need for other adornment.

They'd just dropped off Fredrick, who appeared to be both eager as well as capable. Menefry had few concerns about the Yu'udir working to the best of his abilities as a protector for the newly opened system.

And if he failed, well, Menefry and his crew could always come back and straighten things out. Straighten *him* out.

Menefry was still in charge of security for the ship and crew, though he felt as though the universe, as a whole, had just gotten a lot more secure.

News had reached them that Clayton had committed suicide the week before, watching a film in his private theatre in his rooms aboard the *Dallas* station.

Menefry doubted that Clayton's death had been his own decision. It was entirely possible that he'd willingly downed all those pills himself, but he hadn't come up with the idea on his own. Someone had forced him into it.

Sachiko had, in fact, committed suicide, piloting her private spaceship into a star in a mostly empty system. She'd left behind a lot of details of the work she'd done over the years.

Work which meant that even more of the Cartel board of directors were on the hook for.

Her information hadn't completely pulled the teeth from the Cartel. It still had something of a bite.

However, they no longer controlled the majority of the hyperspace gates. Seemed that once the queens had their portion secured, they were able to reach out and control many of the other gates as well, slipping in underneath the Cartel's stations, able to open and close the tunnels at will.

The Cartel tried to raise a huge alarm over the fact that they were no longer in control.

Fortunately, with most people, the Cartel no longer had any sway. Particularly in the systems where the coming of the queens meant that no one had to pay bribes to access hyperspace. It was now open to everyone, free of charge.

So while there were a few specists who were concerned about those *aliens* taking over, for the most part, it was just business as usual. Nobody noticed or cared that the top level players had changed.

Particularly since there was an entire new market that had just opened, all those Chonchu who could now be traded with.

The queens wanted additional space stations built and had already sent out requests for quotes to various manufacturers.

More credits certainly would grease the wheels of prosperity and silence the naysayers. Even the Goddess approved of commerce.

Menefry looked again up at the statue of the Goddess in Flux. The queens had presented him with a small copy of the Goddess Bringing People Together. He had given it a place of honor in his front rooms. Should he move that statue into here instead?

No, that wasn't right.

But neither was the image of the Goddess in Flux.

Menefry needed something else. A different meditative pose, that would enable him to more closely follow the path the Goddess had clearly set down for him, if he could just open his eyes and trust her steady limbs.

The Goddess in Flux actually felt close to what he wanted. Except that the decision point had already been reached, the crisis passed. They were on their path now.

That was it.

Menefry was no longer static, and a still image of the Goddess was no longer appropriate.

No, he needed a statue of the Goddess in Motion. He already saw it in his mind's eye. One of her legs would be lifted, but instead of pausing, the image would capture her in mid-step, moving forward with a firm goal in mind. Two of her limbs would be reaching back, memories of the past guiding her feet, but the rest would be swinging forward, reaching for the future.

The acknowledgment of the rightness of image settled around Menefry, as if his shell had been lifted a few centimeters from his back and had now locked completely, comfortably, into place.

After all, he was now part of a spaceship, his blood mingled with theirs.

Yes. The Goddess in Motion.

And he would walk with her, as well as his crewmates, guarding the way.

CHAPTER 34

BASIL

BASIL TRIED TO PAY ATTENTION TO THE LATEST chemical experiment that zie was running on zir blood, isolating the new compound added by the queens that the Chonchu could sense.

Zie worked in the secondary engineering room this time instead of down in the engine room as zir other office. The experiments zie was running were all theoretical computer simulations, and not dealing with actual chemicals that the others complained about.

However, zie continued to find zir attention drawn to the dais holding the three tall amber spars of Eleanor, Gawain, and Abban. Though zie didn't see the difference the strips of fabric wrapped around them made, the rest of the crew all thought the fabric improved the Chonchu's appearance dramatically.

Eleanor appeared to notice Basil's distraction. "Is everything all right?" she asked. It was just her at this time. The melodious overtones of one of the queens wasn't present.

"I am," Basil said. Zie sighed and pushed back from zir

workstation, turning to face her. "I was just wondering how *you* were."

As much as Basil tried, zie couldn't sense the Chonchu, not on the same level that they could evidently now sense the rest of the crew. It distressed zim, and honestly, made zim feel something of a failure.

The Oligochuno prided themselves on being able to sense things beyond the other races.

There had to be a way that zie could sense the Chonchu, particularly now that it was built into zir very system.

"We are well," Eleanor assured zim.

"You know, anytime you need to return to the Chonchu system, all you have to do is to let us know," Basil said.

"We know," Gawain replied. "Though that will probably no longer be necessary, not with the queens controlling the hyperspace tunnels."

Basil nodded, having been thinking the same thing. Zie also hadn't been surprised by Gawain being the one replying. That had been happening a lot—it was no longer just Eleanor who interfaced with the crew, but all three of them.

"Good," Basil said. Zie paused, then had to ask, "Has the ability to sense the crewmembers grown stronger? Weaker? Remained the same?"

Abban's halting laugh sounded, but it was Eleanor who replied. "Ever the scientist?"

Basil smiled and waited. Though zie wasn't certain how Eleanor and the others now sensed them, zie did know that they now responded as well to non-verbal signals as if they were in the same room.

"I would stay it's stronger," Gawain added after a slight pause. "That might just be because you're encased in our ship."

Basil also nodded at that. Many, if not most, of the wiring inside of the ship had been replaced with new wires that appeared to have been grown, not manufactured. Though the ship itself was still made of metal and other parts, much of the interior workings were now organic.

Eleanor and the others were now fully in control of the ship. Though she still ceded control to Judit when necessary —while Eleanor could fly the ship, Judit was a better pilot, at least for now.

Basil knew that made Judit nervous occasionally. But mostly she'd gotten over herself.

Basil found zir thoughts darting away. Zie really wasn't focusing well.

"Since we, this ship, are successful, and we've figured out how to be successful, will there be others?" zie asked. "Will the queens continue with Arthur's experiments?"

"Negative," Abban replied. "We are unique."

The pride that filled zir voice surprised Basil.

"What Abban is trying to say is that the only way to achieve what we have with *Eleanor* would be with another bonded crew," Gawain said. "Just a ship, with Chonchu as the drive, isn't enough. They have to have the right people, who would be willing to take the long run with them, aboard."

"Partake in the *Jaimeng* ceremony?" Basil asked.

"Exactly," Eleanor replied. "And there are few who would do that. So for now, we remain unique. The only ship capable of digging its own hyperspace tunnels."

Basil didn't think that was necessarily the worst outcome. Much better for there to be some level of control in terms of access, so that those who were powerful and greedy couldn't just appear in someone else's system and take what they wanted.

"And what about you?" Eleanor asked after a few moments. "What is distracting you so much today?"

"I keep trying to sense you in return," Basil finally admitted. "And I haven't been successful yet."

Eleanor's merry laughter greeted zir confession. "Of course you can't!" she said. "You don't have the necessary sensing organs."

"Oh?" Basil said. "But could I grow them?"

Now, it was Eleanor's turn to sigh. "Possibly. The queens have discussed it. But it would mean you'd be able to sense not merely us, but all of us."

It took Basil a moment to parse Eleanor's meaning.

Zie would be able to sense the queens and the other Chonchu, not just zir crewmates.

That was another level of trust that needed to be gained. And possibly not by all of the crew. They also might not want that level of commitment.

Or responsibility.

Basil thought for a moment, then threw a segment into the ring, as it were.

"I'd like to be able to do that," zie said. "Though I can't speak for the others."

Gawain replied. "We assumed that might be the case. You do work the closest with all of us."

Basil paused, then said, "Thank you."

"For what?" Gawain asked.

Eleanor added, "It should be us thanking you, for keeping us alive, for working so hard at repairing systems that had been designed deliberately to break."

Basil still sometimes wanted to resurrect Masala just to strangle zim. Less so these days.

Though the other Oligochuno would have been as delighted as Basil at the new discoveries they'd made, at how well the queens were now integrated into the hyperspace tunnels.

"You gave me purpose," Basil said after a few moments.

"I was, well, floundering before would be putting it too strongly. But I didn't have a good path to follow. A strong future to inch toward."

"We are symbiotic," Abban said. His harsh laugh echoed through the room. "Ha! Ha! Ha! You and the queens."

Basil bowed zir head at that, then went back to zir current experiments.

Yes, symbiotic. That explained a lot, both of zir relationship with the ship and the Chonchu's relationship with the crew.

They needed each other, to flow and form the shapes as needed. Just a single bond wouldn't do, but multiple ones.

Basil felt zieself settle further into zir segments as zie started to work again with new focus.

Together, they would survive. And thrive.

CHAPTER 35

SAXON

SAXON SAT IN HIS ROOMS ABOARD *ELEANOR*, COMPOSING the latest message that he was going to send to Flora, his sister.

The danger wasn't completely over. The influence of the Cartel was much reduced. Seemed that system governments, now that they had guaranteed access to the hyperspace tunnels and had no fear of being cut off or abandoned, were much less likely to overlook the blatant and egregious law breaking of the Cartel and were bringing them up on charges.

Or, more importantly, breaking the monopolistic stranglehold that the Cartel had on all trade.

There were a few systems who refused to give up their old masters. However, they had lost allies, and were rapidly growing obsolete.

Times had changed. They needed to as well.

Flora, however, would never change. That was just something that Saxon had to accept. She hadn't banished him, cut him off from his family. She had, however, continued to make it clear that he was now considered an outsider.

Saxon tried to not resent that. He really did. He tried to tell himself that it was best for everybody, especially since he had no intention of ever coming back to his home world and settling down there.

Especially now.

Though the others felt no change after the *Jaimeng* ceremony, Saxon occasionally felt something different. A flow of air across his fur, or a sense that someone was there in his empty room.

It didn't surprise him. The Yu'udir were apex predators, no matter how much Humans claimed that spot.

That was just because Humans rarely understood loyalty, exalting the lone cowboy instead of the successful group.

Of all of them, Saxon had probably been the best prepared for Fredrick being able to change alliances, then stick to it.

Saxon hadn't spent a lot of time with Fredrick while he'd been aboard the ship. Fredrick struck Saxon as *slick*, with all that that implied. Fredrick would still get the job done as part of his penance.

Just as now, Saxon paid his, being out here without his family.

No, that wasn't right.

Saxon had a family. It was a family of choice, though, instead of a family of blood.

He'd trust Menefry at his back for any fight. Kim would distract the enemy, or somehow steal all their weapons. Basil would invent something truly evil for villains to fight. Eleanor and her companions would drive any attackers away, using everything in their power to save the rest of their crewmates.

And Judit was still his star, the one he'd hitched his own to. She was his captain, and she would lead the charge wherever they needed to go.

Satisfied, Saxon finished his latest missive and sent it off, no longer feeling the need to beg for understanding or forgiveness.

His family understood his choices and his life.

Or at least, his real family did.

CHAPTER 36

JUDIT

"Ow!" Judit said as she stubbed her toe, leaving the gym after a long, sweaty workout and heading back toward her rooms.

She opened her mouth to swear in Hungarian, then paused. Considered.

It had been a long, *long* time since she'd banged into anything on the ship, since Saxon had asked in that dry voice of his if she was being graceful as always.

"Eleanor?" Judit asked, studying the floor in front of her.

It hadn't *necessarily* all been her fault. There did appear to be a slight bump there.

"Oh! Sorry!" Eleanor replied immediately.

The bump that Judit saw suddenly smoothed itself.

Judit couldn't help her shudder. The ship was more *alive* than she liked admitting, more grown and less manufactured.

"Is Basil with you?" Judit said, words and conversation bubbling up inside of her.

"No, zie is down in the engine room, in zir second office," Eleanor said.

"I'd like to come visit, then," Judit said. "If that's okay?"

"Of course!" Eleanor said. "You are always welcome."

Judit shook her head as she hurried along the corridors, heading toward the secondary engine room.

While she knew that she was welcome, she still wanted to always, *always*, treat Eleanor, Gawain, and Abban like people who had a choice as to whether or not someone came storming into their room or not.

Eleanor had assured Judit on more than one occasion that she still had control of the door that separated the secondary engine room from the primary one, and could always slam it shut and keep it locked if need be.

Judit still tried to always ask, to never assume that the Chonchu wanted company.

The secondary engine room looked so much better than the first time she'd entered it, when so many of the tubes had been broken: both those used to carry the nutrients that the Chonchu needed and the ones that kept the room cool.

Now, the room was clean and ordered, all the tubes the same steel color. Basil's plant hung in the corner. It appeared to be happy, as additional vines dangled down the sides. The room still had that smell of chemicals and algae, some combination of manufactured and grown.

"What was on your mind?" Eleanor asked as soon as Judit entered the small space.

Judit paused. Instead of taking the time to order everything into a coherent speech, she allowed herself to just spew.

"We have this ship. We are part of you, and you're part of us. You needed that. But now, well, what do we do?" Judit said. "You don't need me. You don't need a captain or a pilot. Not really."

And maybe that was the true heart of the issue, as Judit felt her gut wrench.

"But we do—" Eleanor started to say.

"No, no you don't. You're becoming a better pilot. You'll surpass me one of these days. What do you need me for?"

"The crew needs a captain," Gawain said gently.

Judit grimaced. She only vaguely fit that part. She tried to run the ship mostly in a democratic manner, asking for input and getting the team to vote on things.

Sure, she had to put it all together, but it wasn't really what got her up in the mornings. Made her reach for her coffee instead of turning over and going back to sleep.

"The Cartel's actively working itself into irrelevance," Judit said. It had actually been fun watching them self-destruct. There had been some unforeseen consequences, and a few systems had seen violence. For the most part, though, the coup had been bloodless.

"The queens have been funding us over and above what I can make for us hauling cargo," Judit continued. It had been her one job, something she'd defined herself by for years. Decades, even. And she would be the first to admit that it had been nice to not have to be scrambling for credits all the time.

The cost of the chemicals to maintain Eleanor, Gawain, and Abban were always going to leave them strapped. So the queens had given them a generous stipend so they could keep flying.

Judit looked around bleakly. What else was there left for her?

"There are always problems to solve," Eleanor said quietly. "Injustices to be righted."

Judit blinked, taken aback.

"Talk to me," she said as she felt everything shift.

"The queens can see into almost every system now," Eleanor said. "And there are a lot of places that are not peaceful or equitable."

"I see," Judit said slowly. She'd been angry at the Cartel for so long.

It would be good to be able to shift that rage toward something else. To continue the good fight.

"Can you provide me with a list of systems that the queens would like for us to visit?" Judit asked as her soul and her being rearranged themselves.

"There are a lot of them," Eleanor warned.

"That's fine," Judit said. "We'll come up with a ranking system later."

She could do this. It was a task that was unusually suited for someone like her. As well as the ship, being able to sneak into and out of systems without anyone the wiser.

Judit turned and left engineering, going back to her rooms to shower and prepare herself to tackle the problems in the rest of the universe.

To make prosperity Universal. Equity. To be a voice for those who had none.

And it was awesome that there were many of them. Judit was looking forward to a long, long career. A long run of doing more good, as it were.

One day at a time. One planet at a time. One system at a time.

Or even, *egyszerre egy kecske*: one goat at a time.

READ MORE!

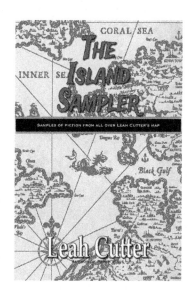

Are you a traveler? Do you enjoy exploring strange new worlds, new cultures, new people?

Journey into the various lands envisioned by Leah R Cutter.

Sign up for my newsletter and I'll start you on your travels with a free copy of my book, *The Island Sampler*.

I will never spam you or use your email for nefarious purposes. You can also unsubscribe at any time.

http://www.LeahCutter.com/newsletter/

ABOUT THE AUTHOR

Leah Cutter writes page-turning fiction in exotic locations, such as a magical New Orleans, the ancient Orient, Hungary, the Oregon coast, rural Kentucky, Seattle, Minneapolis, and many others.

She writes literary, fantasy, mystery, science fiction, and horror fiction. Her short fiction has been published in magazines like *Alfred Hitchcock's Mystery Magazine* and *Talebones*, anthologies like Fiction River, and on the web. Her long fiction has been published both by New York publishers as well as small presses.

Find Leah's books on Knotted Road Press at (www.KnottedRoadPress.com)

Follow her blog at www.LeahCutter.com.

Reviews

It's true. Reviews help me sell more books. If you've enjoyed this story, please consider leaving a review of it on your favorite site.

Come someplace new...

Are you a traveler? Do you enjoy exploring strange new worlds, new cultures, new people?

Journey into the various lands envisioned by Leah Cutter.

Sign up for my newsletter and I'll start you on your travels with a free copy of my book, *The Island Sampler*.

I will never spam you or use your email for nefarious purposes. You can also unsubscribe at any time.

http://www.LeahCutter.com/newsletter/

ABOUT KNOTTED ROAD PRESS

Knotted Road Press fiction specializes in dynamic writing set in mysterious, exotic locations.

Knotted Road Press non-fiction publishes autobiographies, business books, cookbooks, and how-to books with unique voices.

Knotted Road Press creates DRM-free ebooks as well as high-quality print books for readers around the world.

With authors in a variety of genres including literary, poetry, mystery, fantasy, and science fiction, Knotted Road Press has something for everyone.

Knotted Road Press
www.KnottedRoadPress.com

Printed in Great Britain
by Amazon

44440609R00126